# MISADVENTURES OF A MIDDLE AGED RUNAWAY

Jeanne Shevlin Gates

*Thanks to my friends Carol, Dee, & Kay for listening
to my stories. Many thanks to my writing group:
Carol, Denis, & Lenny for all your guidance.*

MISADVENTURES OF A MIDDLE-AGED RUNAWAY

by Jeanne Shevlin Gates

© 2022 Gates

TABLE OF CONTENTS

## PROLOGUE

As I traveled through life, I soon came to the realization that I never wanted to look back and say, "I wish I had done that."

Going to exotic places doesn't just happen. It takes planning and desire. Books and magazines have information about any trip imaginable. Just turn that first page.

I didn't start my life expecting I would travel the world. As a child in rural New Hampshire, going to the next state was an exciting experience. It wasn't until my fifties that opportunities presented themselves. I grabbed them and took off for places unknown with a sense of adventure I didn't know I possessed.

I hope this collection of stories inspires you to explore outside your comfort zone. Each one of these chapters are precious pieces of my gifted life.

# CHAPTER 1 MEXICO

DECEMBER 1992

Only a matter of days after turning fifty, my best friend, Kay, and I planned a trip to Cancun, Mexico. At that time, I was working as an RN in the emergency room in Myrtle Beach, South Carolina. I enjoyed emergency nursing, had lots of friends and an active social life. Other than short trips many years ago, this trip was long overdue. Lying on the beach in sunshine, reading a good book and having no schedule sounded good.

Kay is an expert planner and bargain hunter. She found an inexpensive one-week tour over the Christmas holidays. We would celebrate my birthday and leave winter behind.

We shopped for bargains. We needed bathing suits, beach hats, sandals and everything related to tourist travel. We even studied some Spanish we might need. We memorized, *si si senor, uno cervesa por favor,* and *a donde es el bano.* Don't check my Spanish because it's probably wrong.

The night prior to our leaving, Kay and I spent time on the phone making sure we had our boarding passes, passports, and money. We knew that we had packed too many clothes, but we would probably change two or three times a day.

I drove to Kay's house in the morning, early as usual. Kay was running late, as usual. We both had one large suitcase, a carry on and purse. We were nervous when they weighed our bags. Thank goodness summer clothes are light.

The trip was short and when we stepped off onto the tarmac, the warmth of the sun on my face promised at least one week of summer. We had shed our winter sweaters and slacks for sleeveless tops and sandals. When we left Myrtle Beach, it was forty-five degrees and in Mexico it was a delightful eighty-five.

Alex, our assigned tour guide, met our travel group as we passed through customs. Kay had been in touch with Alex several times prior to the trip so they were like old friends. He had arranged his schedule to take us on a tour of the local market and a sightseeing trip during the week.

Checking in at the hotel as fast as possible, we found our room, threw open the suitcases, dressed in outfits for an afternoon excursion, exchanged US dollars for local money at the front desk, and we were off to the bus stop. Destination Hard Rock Café.

As all great vacation stories begin, it just so happened that there were six handsome guys from Detroit on the bus. They also had just arrived and were on their way to Senor Frogs. How could we say no when they asked us to join them? If you've never been to Senor Frogs that's a shame. Their large-shuttered windows overlook a pond, and when patrons become too rowdy, they are tossed out into the pond. Fortunately for us, this usually occurred on wild evenings. As we entered it was early afternoon and the rock music was blasting with a "move your body" beat.

After an hour of drinking and dancing, a voice from our group yelled, "Hey! How about we all find Hard Rock Café?" As we gathered on the sidewalk, one of the guys lit up a "happy" cigarette. I crossed the street along with Ken, and we walked apart from the group. He called to his friends, "Jeanne and I will meet you at Hard Rock." He received smiles and a thumbs up from his friends. Ken looked at me and asked, "So, what do you do back home?"

"Well, I'm a nurse and have frequent drug testing. I also prefer not to go to jail in Mexico. What do you do?"

With a big smile, he whispered, I'm with DEA.

We shared a conspiratorial laugh. It was a short distance to Hard Rock. We found the group already there ordering drinks and lunch. Ken and the gang were having a great time when we slipped away unnoticed, paid our bill and bought T-shirts for ourselves and friends.

On our way back to the hotel, Kay suggested, "How about getting dressed up? We can take the bus into town, have dinner, and I can show you how to haggle on prices in one of the jewelry stores."

Kay loved to brag about being able to haggle, so I agreed to the tutorial. We found a cute outdoor dining area with bright umbrellas. We ordered tequilas and the special, two tacos for the price of one. Feasting on warm corn chips and tasty salsa, enjoying our tequilas, we soaked up the atmosphere. There were six upside-down tequila shot glasses on the table when we left.

Kay spied a jewelry store near the restaurant, we headed that way. As we entered the store, a salesman approached us asking if we were looking for anything special. Kay politely answered, "No, we're just browsing, thank you."

As we walked around, Kay picked up a bracelet and asked the price. When he told her, she said, "too much," put it down, and continued to look around. She returned to the same bracelet. He suggested a lower price and she just shook her head. Walking around for a few more minutes, she asked him if he would take her offer for the bracelet as we were leaving.

We both jumped when he yelled. "Get out. Get out. You Americans. You want to pay too cheap!"

As we walked briskly away, we started to laugh. I looked at her. "Wow, that didn't go so well, did it?"

Kay just gave me a look that said, "Don't go there."

It was getting dark, and we were nervous about being in

an area that may not be safe. We waited at the bus stop and took the next bus back to the hotel. We were tired. With a hangover in the making, we finished unpacking. Tomorrow was a long bus trip to Chichen Itza, the Mayan ruins.

Our group had already boarded the bus and Alex was standing outside with the driver. We were the last to arrive. We got a few looks as we boarded. Kay looked at me and whispered, "What! We were only about five minutes late. What's the big deal."

"Better check your watch. We were fifteen minutes late. I'm going to start telling you we need to be ready one hour before the real time." All I got was a rolling of her eyes as she found our seats. Since we were the last ones on, we were in the rear of the bus. I didn't even make a comment.

As we traveled through the isolated countryside, Kay said she thought it looked a lot like the desert in our southwest. There was lots of activity in the villages we passed. Except for the sombreros, it could have been a small rural town anywhere.

The Mayan ruins were more remarkable than I could have imagined. Kay and I climbed the tallest pyramid. I'm afraid of high places and had to sit down on the top, too scared to stand. I gingerly slid down the narrow steps on my butt. Our guide pointed out large flat rocks used for virgin sacrifices. We laid on the stones for a test, but nothing happened. The many small pyramids and stone buildings had small holes in the wall, lining up with the sun to predict times of the year. The Mayans were very advanced in astrology and math. Some think that they have been assisted by extraterrestrials. Personally, I think it may be a possibility.

Exhausted from a long day, we decided to relax at the pool in the morning. We signed up for a scuba diving lesson, but we had difficulty clearing our masks and popping our ears as we descended. We flunked. Embarrassed but not discouraged, we stopped at our favorite hotel bar. Kay tucked a flower behind her ear, crossed her legs and smiled at our favorite bartender, "Pedro".

"*Buenos dias," Pedro. Dos cervesas, por favor,*" she said. Then added, "*Frio*". I can only imagine what goes through Pedro's mind when tourists try to speak Spanish. He was sweet and never made us feel anything but adored. He pointed to Kay's flower and said, we think, "pretty".

He served us two cold beers, smiled widely, displaying a golden front tooth, and looked longingly at Kay. We would visit him often during our stay.

We enjoyed a lunch at the hotel. Trying to avoid salads, we had hamburgers, French fries and bottled water. At my suggestion, we took one antibiotic pill daily to avoid GI problems. So far, it was working, but we were being careful.

Alex picked us up in the hotel lobby. He had offered to take us to the local market this afternoon. It was busy and festive with bright umbrellas and lots of small shops for tourists. He knew many of the vendors and Kay didn't have to use her bargaining skills. We stopped at kiosks selling food to sample local cuisine. Kay got carried away and even tried a milk drink. I was trying to stick to cooked food. About two hours into our market experience, I turned to Alex and said, "Where is the nearest restroom?"

Excusing myself for the rest of the market tour, I walked the short distance back to the hotel, praying that I would make it to my room. The GI problems persisted along with a fever. When Kay returned, I excused myself from dinner with her and Alex. After some fluids and Tylenol, I was good as new in the morning.

A day at the beach was decided upon for the next day. Just a relaxing dip in the ocean and some sunshine. Rather than stay at our hotel, we traveled by bus to a luxury hotel. Pretending we were hotel guests, we passed through the lobby to the beach. With a couple of comfy beach chairs, we were content. Kay commented on the red flags flying along the beach and thought they were for a celebration. We learned what they were for, but too late.

Laughing and splashing in the shallow water, deciding our evening, we began returning to our beach chairs and turned to walk out of the water. Just knee deep, neither of us was able to fight the pressure pulling us backwards. We got deeper into waves which were now breaking over our heads and sucking us under. We were being pulled out farther and within seconds, we were separated. We were in a rip tide. I could see Kay being swept away quickly. Green waves crashed over my head, I went under, came up, took a breath and was back under. I just knew I was going to drown, so the next wave, I waved my arms to get help. I had only a few more waves before I would run out of strength.

A brown face appeared before me. I turned so he could grab me. When he did, I kicked as hard as I could. Once on the beach, Kay suddenly appeared with a lifeguard and flopped down on the sand beside me. We just held hands as the tears streamed down our cheeks.

The two lifeguards, teenagers, had jeopardized their lives to save us. One said, "Don't you know what the red flags mean?"

The other said, "It's okay if you want to give us money."

How much money do you give someone for saving your life? We gave them all our cash, saving only bus fare. It was about fifty dollars and not enough. We cried on the way back to our hotel. We really needed a drink and Pedro served us tequila. We were so relieved that we were alive. I said to Kay, "You know, you and I would have been two unidentified American tourists on a slab in the morgue. It would have been days or weeks before they figured out who we were."

"You're right. We had no ID with us. I don't know about you, but I'm going to appreciate every day for the rest of my life." That got Kay crying again. We had another tequila.

We felt bad about not being able to give the lifeguards enough money. She wrote a letter to the hotel, telling them of the heroism of the lifeguards. She also had the local radio station announce our heroic rescue on the news that evening. A couple of days later we were able to find out from the hotel manager when our heroes would be on duty. We found them, gave them twenty dollars each and brought them T-shirts.

The first morning of the rest of our lives, we were subdued. It was a good day to lay in the hammocks along the beach, read, and visit Pedro. Suntanned and relaxed, we took a cab to Daddy O's. After listening to good music and enjoying a delicious seafood dinner, we were content to relax in our room. It was Christmas Eve but really didn't feel like a celebration. We called our families to wish them a Merry Christmas. We never mentioned our harrowing experience.

Ready for a fun night out, Planet Hollywood sounded great. We spent a long time dressing up. When we arrived, we were not disappointed. This was a happening place. Clothing worn by stars was displayed on walls. A long shiny wood bar was filled with noisy customers. Luckily, we found two seats together. As we sat talking and absorbing the energy in the room, Kay leaned over, "Hey, Jeanne. There's a bald guy at the end of the bar giving you the once over. Bald. Just how you like them."

As I turned to look, he was talking to a friend. When I turned back to Kay, she told me he was looking at me again. I turned and Mr. Bald Man and I locked eyes. We both smiled. He and his friend approached us. It didn't take long to find out that they were from Italy and did not speak English. Sergio, my bald friend, spoke a little French and Spanish. I knew a little of each language and had fun trying to communicate. Sergio was a pharmacist and Pino was a model. Oh, yes, he was gorgeous. I would buy whatever he was wearing. He zoned in on Kay who speaks nothing but English, but that didn't seem to matter.

They asked us if we would like to accompany them to a nightclub called The Cave. As we entered, the lighting was dim, and the inside was circular like a cave. Tables were tucked along the walls. The immense dance floor with ornate parquet wood was worn smooth. Dancers packed the dance floor, and the music was lively and Latin.

We used a lot of sign language, laughed, and enjoyed a pitcher of Sangria spiced with cherries and oranges. Lured to the dance floor by a long conga line we joined the snake like dancing around the floor, stopping by the stage where someone squirted tequila into our mouths from a goatskin? We'll never top this Christmas night.

Plans for the next day fell through when Sergio returned home for a family emergency. Before he left, he made sure that we knew Pino wanted to join us the next day for a ferry trip to Isla Mujeres. Kay and I picked him up at his hotel. Somehow, we all managed to get through the ferry ride and found a nice beach to snorkel.

Arriving on the beach, we found a Speedo clad body builder getting a lot of attention from the female sunbathers. His name was Tarzan. Kay and I had our picture taken with him. That is not to say that Pino was not getting a good share of the attention from the fairer sex. He did cut one fine figure in his Speedo. We spent time hanging out on the beach and then snorkeling in the clear lagoon. I managed to find out that he was returning to Rome the next day. He asked Kay if she would like to go to dinner with him that evening. She said yes. I asked her about his not speaking English. She had no comment, just smiled. As a side note, a few weeks after we returned to Myrtle Beach, she received an envelope with modeling pictures from Pino. Wow. She wouldn't give me one to put on my refrigerator.

As this would be our last night in Mexico, we wanted to stay up all night and enjoy the sunset and sunrise. We found a nightclub where we danced our feet off. When the bar closed, we found a nearby beach and strolled until the sun came up against a pastel pink and gray sky.

We took a cab back to the hotel, bypassing the front desk, planning to pack for our afternoon flight. The front desk would have our bills completed so I offered to pick them up. When I arrived at the desk, the clerk asked me, "Are you the American girls leaving today?"

"Yes. Is there a problem?" I had a bad feeling.

"Your flight left already. They left a message in your room yesterday telling you about the earlier flight time. Did you not find the message?"

"No. I'll be right back with my friend." I rushed to the room and told Kay the bad news. We returned to the desk where Kay became undone, crying, telling the clerk that we didn't have money to pay for extra nights. The manager, hearing the commotion, took over and assured us that we would not have to pay for two nights, and they would supply breakfasts. However, we would be expected to be on the early morning flight back to Myrtle Beach on Monday.

We agreed and returned to our room with relief. I can't really say that we were unhappy about two more days in Mexico. Checking our room, we found a slip of pink paper with a notice of the early flight. It's not surprising that we didn't find it under all the clothes strewn on the floor.

Two more days of beach time was a treat. We spent time with Pedro between sunbathing, swimming, and reading. We felt too guilty to do the nightclub thing but did walk to the local market and enjoy meals out on the weekend.

At four in the morning on Monday, our phone rang. It was the front desk reminding us that our flight time was at eight and the shuttle would leave the hotel at five thirty. I think they had probably watched us all weekend to make sure that we were back in the hotel Sunday night.

What a vacation. We relaxed, got a tan, flunked scuba diving class, met some interesting guys and cheated destiny. We'll talk about this trip for a long time.

# CHAPTER 2
# TOURING EUROPE

1993

I was asked to be the maid of honor at the wedding of my best friend, Kay. Her wedding would take place in Birmingham, England. Since I wasn't invited on the honeymoon, I had to entertain myself for seven days. She suggested a train trip, and her fiancée, Simon, obtained train schedules for England, Scotland, and the Channel Islands.

At fifty-one, I had never spent a night alone in another state, not to mention in another country. I've never eaten alone at a restaurant. Taking a train, finding lodging, and getting lost terrified me.

I practiced being alone before the trip. Spending the day at the mall, I visited shops, had lunch, enjoyed a good movie, shopped until dinnertime, and on the way home treated myself to a delicious dinner in a nice restaurant. I brought a book to read to ease my tension about being alone. Walking into the movie theater before the lights went out, was uncomfortable. Maybe the next time will be easier.

To prepare for the trip, I read brochures and bought a guidebook. I dusted off a large map from my office and traced my trip. Choosing days at each city and interesting sites to visit were circled. A Frommer's guidebook helped me make reservations at hotels. I was ready.

Kay arranged for us to stay at a hotel near the airport

the night before our direct flight to Heathrow. The hotel offered shuttle services to the airport and allowed parking in their lot while we traveled.

Before daylight the next morning, we were at the curb with all our suitcases. Kay had an extra suitcase for her wedding wardrobe. She would be having a civil ceremony and then a formal wedding in a medieval church.

We traveled first class using Kay's frequent flyer miles. It was my initial experience in first class. Plenty of room to rest during the night flight and a nice dinner with complimentary wine is the way to travel.

Simon was waiting for us as we exited customs. We both laughed when we saw him hopping up and down in the crowd with the sign, MRS. HARDING, a big smile on his handsome face. Our luggage barely fit in his tiny car. With a suitcase on my lap in the back seat I slid every time he screeched around a turn on the narrow road. I squeezed my eyes shut at intersections when he drove on the left instead of the right.

Simon's family welcomed us. This was the first time any of them had met Americans. I felt a sense of accountability for my behavior.

The next afternoon, a small group of family and friends attended the civil ceremony at the town hall. Simon's best friend George and his wife were there. George had a band during the Beatles era and some big hits. That evening, we gathered at a local bar where George played the piano and entertained us all with his huge personality and talent. I recognized several of his songs.

On the wedding day, a Rolls-Royce with a big red ribbon on the hood took us to the church. The medieval church dating from the 1300s had stained-glass windows reflecting prism lights from the sun as Kay walked down the aisle. The ceremony was solemn by the surroundings and uplifting due to the occasion. The reception party was in full swing when we arrived. Everyone was dancing to rock and roll music on a huge dance floor. The food was delicious and never ending. Guinness flowed until dawn.

After staying that night with Simon's parents, they drove me to the local train station as Kay and Simon were departing for their honeymoon in London. My train trip to Edinburgh began with a siren blasting at the station and everyone running. I heard someone say there was a bomb threat. Strangely I wasn't scared, just following the crowd while we all waited for the all clear signal so we could board.

I booked a room in a small hotel near the train station in the center of town. As I stood on the platform, a drizzle of rain began. As I left the station, I could see the hotel. It took only a few moments to get there and check in. My room on the second floor was small but the overstuffed chairs and cheerful bed cover were homey. A bay window overlooked a park.

I changed into jeans and a warm sweater and visited the park. A large bulletin board advertised local events and one caught my eye. A Kaylee was being held tonight at a local restaurant. It was a ceremony of  haggis with dinner and dancing.  I jotted down the time and address, spending the rest of the afternoon exploring the city. I called for a taxi to pick me up at the hotel at six.

A ruddy faced smiling driver opened the taxi door for me, asking, "Are you the lassie going to the Kaylee?"

I replied, "Yes. I have a lot of questions and maybe you can help me. What is haggis?"

"Well, It's the stomach of a sheep stuffed with liver and onions that's a delicacy here in Scotland. They'll be a whole celebration before the meal dedicated to the haggis. Have you ever heard the pipes, lassie?"

"Only in thc movies," I replied.

"Tonight, my friend is playing the pipes and will be practicing on the patio behind the restaurant. He'll be pleasured to give you a private concert."

And he did. In full dress of plaid skirt and shawl, he marched up and down the driveway behind the restaurant, playing the bagpipes. It was wonderful. The performance made me feel like I had traveled back hundreds of years.

Seating was at a long table, family style, and I sat with a local couple who explained the entire ceremony. I did try the haggis but buried it in a mound of delicious potatoes. The gentleman asked me to dance. The steps were like the square dances we performed in high school. What an amazing evening.

The next day I toured the city and visited a castle dating back to the iron age. The chapel inside had leather books where the name of every Scottish soldier ever lost in battle was handwritten on the pages. Refracting light through the immense stained-glass windows gave an aura of peace.

Off to Glasgow the next morning. On arrival I asked directions from the stationmaster, and he offered to give me a ride to my hotel I booked ahead. He insisted that it was on his way home.

He was a talkative elderly gentleman with wisps of white hair under his cap. He drove me through Glasgow, telling me about his city. He smiled and tipped his cap as I left his car, and said, "Have a nice trip, lassie." My hotel was not as nice as the one in Edinburgh. Eating in their restaurant that night, I didn't leave the hotel, not feeling safe in the area. Tomorrow I would be in Bath and visit Stonehenge.

The train ride to the Bath station was short and I was met with thick fog. At the station I asked the clerk for directions to a local hotel. This small town had many hotels, so I made a reservation at one that was highly recommended.

My room on the second floor was warm and inviting.

The hotel restaurant had a small pub playing local lively music. Finding a table away from other diners, I enjoyed fish and chips and a Guinness. Declining desert, I tapped my foot to the music as I enjoyed a second beer. I slept very well. Tomorrow I would tour the town and Stonehenge.

The fog was too thick for traveling to the Stonehenge site, so I toured the town, visiting the ancient baths and shopping. This afternoon I would take the hovercraft to Jersey, one of the Channel Islands. George, Simon's best man, played piano in a bar there.

Arriving at the ticket booth for my trip across the English Channel to the island of Jersey, I was told there were no more tickets. After a lot of whining and begging, I boarded with ticket in hand. The boat looked like an oversized pontoon boat with a skirt that travels just above the surface of the water. The channel was rough and each time the boat hit a wave the passengers were jerked up and down. My return the next day will be on a ferry.

The tourist center in the lobby was manned with several people. I asked a gentleman behind the counter, "Is there a hotel that you would recommend?" He smiled and kindly asked where I was from, and how long was I staying. He assured me that the taxi would take me to a very nice hotel. When the taxi arrived, he spoke to the driver, and I was taken to a luxury hotel.

The owner met me in the lobby. "Welcome. The tourist center told me you need a room for tonight. Please follow me and we'll get you signed in." My room overlooked the ocean. The ornate furniture, especially the bed with a thick duvet was inviting. After freshening up, I returned to the lobby and asked for a dinner recommendation. He said he would have a cab pick me up at seven thirty and would take me to his friend's restaurant.

He must have called ahead as a nicely dressed stately man met me as I arrived. He welcomed me to his restaurant and had a waiter seat me in a secluded section on the deck with a sunset view. I ordered the seafood specialty and enjoyed the meal and wine. As I left, I asked the owner who was standing at the entrance, "Do you know where the Seaside Bar is? I'm a friend of George who plays the piano there."

"Really. You're a friend of George?  I'll walk you down there. It's only a short distance. He took my arm and we walked along a sidewalk with the ocean breeze on our faces. Arriving at the bar, he greeted the bar owner and introduced me. George was not performing that night. However, the owners of the restaurant and the bar invited me for drinks. The three of us enjoyed drinks and pleasant conversation until midnight.

The next morning, I took a ferry back to the port instead of the hydrofoil. I planned to meet the honeymooners in London and did not look forward to two train rides to get there. They met me at the train station and took me to their hotel. We had lots to catch up on and stayed in the restaurant for hours enjoying stories about our adventures.

While they were still sleeping in the morning, I decided to take a walk around the block. I got lost within minutes because the streets are random. While wandering around, I found a store selling tickets to the Phantom of the Opera. Being required to buy tickets in bundles of two, I bought four tickets, using the balance on my credit card.

I did find my way back to the hotel with some help of locals. Kay and Simon were so excited about the tickets. We were off on an exciting evening and had no problem selling my extra ticket. We were enthralled by *Phantom of the Opera*. I relived the scenes all night in my dreams and hummed the music for weeks.

Simon, Kay, and I traveled home together. We'll have unbelievable stories and pictures to last a lifetime.

# CHAPTER 3 VIRGIN ISLANDS

1994

Landed in paradise! The view from the plane caused a physical reaction. Relief that I was here, amazement at the beauty of the clear green water, and anxiety about a new job. The Virgin Islands beckoned and here I am.

Just a few months ago, I was trudging away in cold temperatures at my old job in the emergency room in South Carolina. I thought I was content, not happy, but living my life. I had begun to date Bill, a local business owner. After spending time together, we found we had a lot in common, especially a love of travel.

The thrill of working in the emergency room had never dulled over the last thirty years. Every day was new with excitement mixed with routine. I even had a part time job as an agency nurse, hiring out at various hospitals around the state on the weekends. The extra money was nice, and the different hospitals provided a stimulus for new professional experiences.

One day, while reading a magazine during some rare down time, there it was. Travel nurses needed in the U.S. Virgin Islands. I picked up the phone and called the 1-800 number. I received the multiple page employment application and began the process. Fingerprints, documents, copies of licenses from multiple states. It took two weeks to gather the needed information. In March, six weeks later, I received the news that

I had a job in the hospital emergency room in St. Thomas, U.S.V.I.

Telling my friends and family was interesting. Their reactions were not what I expected. My daughter was not happy about my decision. The first thing she said was, "Mom, you can't just up and leave everything." My best friend said, "Is it safe there? What will you do with all the things in your apartment? Will you make enough money?" My brother, a person who never travels said, "Good for you, Jeanne. Have a great time. Take a lot of pictures." The girls at work thought I had lost my mind. They were curious about the emergency room where I would be working. Nothing was going to stop me from the adventure of my lifetime.

When I told Bill about my decision, he smiled and said, "I can be packed tomorrow." In two weeks, we were standing in line at the airport.

I contacted the post office in St. Thomas to alert them that I would be mailing twenty large cartons. My name would be on the cartons, addressed to the post office. They contained clothing, books, kitchen items and Bill's tools. He planned to use his skills as a mechanic and open a small shop. We would pick them up on arrival, and I gave them the date we expected to be there.

The taxi ride from the St. Thomas airport was like a roller coaster. The roads were narrow, the taxi drove on the wrong side of the road, and it was uphill with hairpin curves. I was asking myself how I could ever drive here.

Our new home was on the north end of the island. The travel nursing agency provided a stipend for housing. We selected an apartment on the second floor in a four-unit building. It overlooked the ocean and small islands nearby. All windows and doors to the immense porch were open to warm ocean breezes.

Two other traveling nursing couples soon arrived. One

couple, Sue, and Alex, were both nurses. The other couple, Denise was a nurse and her boyfriend, a chef. As it happened, all three girls were working in the emergency room. Alex was hired as a supervisor nurse on the medical units. He looked like a linebacker, and I expected that he would not have a problem keeping order. That first night, we all sat out on the porch, drinking beer from a nearby store. The consensus was to make the most of being in the islands and have lots of fun.

Our first day, Bill and I called a taxi to take us to find a car rental. The rental was easy but obtaining a local driving license was third world. Everything here required paperwork. If you wanted anything completed, there were men for hire to take your papers through the back door and get them signed. The driver's license examination book was tattered, dirty and written partially in English and some other language. The day I took the test, there were two white off islanders, and we were the only two to pass the test.

After picking up our containers from the post office that first day, shopping for groceries was next on our list. There was a large wholesale store where we found everything we needed except rum. That we found in a liquor store and made sure we got the largest size of Captain Morgan. We returned home to get all in order. I started work in two days.

I'll share my secret for the best rum punch drinks. After many attempts, I found the perfect blend. First, five ice cubes in a glass. Pour the rum until it covers the ice. Add a 50-50 mixture of guava and pineapple juice to near the top of the glass. Add two maraschino cherries and one teaspoon of cherry juice. Our porch was rum punch central in the evenings.

Bill dropped me off the first morning behind the hospital in a small parking lot. A large cow was staked out on a piece of grass near the back entrance. It wasn't difficult to find the ER since the hospital was very small. The nurses on duty that day were friendly but a little guarded. Many were traveling nurses from the mainland who decided to stay on permanently. Sue, Denise, and I spent a lot of time that day shooting looks at each other and rolling our eyeballs. I won't go into detail about the hospital, but on that first day, I prayed that I would not get sick.

This feeling was reinforced that afternoon when a couple was brought in by ambulance. As many tourists had already done, they had probably been on the wrong side of the road and hit another car head on. They were in a rented open Jeep. The man had only minor injuries, but his girlfriend was not as fortunate. Her knees hit the dashboard and dislocated both of her hips, fracturing one of them. Having orthopedic surgery here was not an option. He spent hours trying to find air transportation to Florida. It was incredibly expensive. She was finally transported that evening. The next morning, I obtained air ambulance insurance.

Many evenings, the six of us would meet at a local restaurant for drinks and local food. There was a ferry to St. John, a nearby island. It was seventy percent national forest and had one small village. The stores there had local crafts, island clothing, good food and Pusser's Bar. We spent a lot of time there on weekends.

They served a drink that tasted like a chocolate milkshake. It was lethal. It contained several liqueurs. After one, when you stood, you found yourself listing just a little off plumb. We knew about the drink but loved to watch unwary tourists throw back a few while sitting down and then attempt to stand up. One afternoon we all laughed as we watched a young man stand and then slowly lean until he defied gravity.

The beaches on St. John are plentiful, vacant and look postcard perfect. We had the best snorkeling places in the universe and beaches to relax on in solitude. The reefs were shallow, the water clear to thirty feet and the fish plentiful. The beaches on St. Thomas were also beautiful. We had to be careful never to be alone as a couple on a beach. Unfortunately, drugs had invaded the islands. We sometimes ran out of rape kits in the ER.

Bill and I decided to take scuba diving classes. After my near drowning in Mexico last year, I was a little nervous. In class, I had trouble clearing my mask. The will to dive overcame my fear, and the day came for my first dive. Bill was a great dive partner. He was patient and attentive; always making sure my equipment was in good order and staying nearby for support. The dive was to twenty feet in clear water.

The plan was to learn to jump in, give the ok signal and descend to the bottom. When they say "fat floats" they are not kidding. I have a lot of body fat and realized that I needed about thirteen pounds of weights around my waist to be able to descend. Otherwise, my butt floats to the surface. Too much information? Nearing the bottom, I panicked. Some divers were using a rope to descend, and I decided I was going up. It was irrational because I was not going to drown. My regulator was in my mouth with plenty of air but in my mind, I had to get up to the surface. I clawed my way over other divers.

Bill followed me up and sat with me on the boat. We reviewed our instructions from class. I knew that if I didn't go right back down, I would miss out on scuba diving. The next attempt was smoother, and despite fear, I learned to use my breathing to be more buoyant and to relax and enjoy the wonderful weightless feeling. After that day, Bill and I took every opportunity to dive or snorkel.

Virgin Gorda, in the British Virgin Islands was just a ferry ride away. It was the most beautiful place I had ever visited. In my mind, I could see myself living there forever on my forty-foot sailboat anchored offshore, relaxing on the white sand beach, snorkeling, or scuba diving in the clear green waters.

The topography looks like a giant had a handful of house sized boulders, threw them up into the air, and they landed like marbles. Boulders littered the entire landscape with many piled up on one end of the largest beach. The white fine beach sand was lapped by green transparent water. Warm breezes kept the temperature just right. It would be one of our favorite places to visit.

Another favorite island in the BVI was Tortola. On Sundays, we would take the ferry over and have brunch on a restaurant pier. Boats were moored nearby, bobbing in their wooden slots. Catamarans were my favorite. We even talked about buying one to live in, able to sail away at our leisure. Looking back, I'm glad that I wasn't hasty about that wish.

Life moves at a slower pace in the islands. Life was good. Being a diver now, I expressed interest in the hyperbaric chamber at the hospital. The director was a doctor from Duke, an expert in hyperbaric medicine. We were lucky to have him there as this chamber was the only one available for divers in trouble other than Florida. I requested to be transferred there part-time and on call.

An old submarine the size of a car was found in a ditch on the island and lovingly transformed into a hyperbaric unit. It had two cots inside and a double entrance on one end. On entering, the outer door is closed, the pressure adjusted to the inner chamber, then the inner chamber could be entered. The time a diver had to stay inside was determined by timetables used by the Navy.

My first patient was a twenty-year-old Puerto Rico diver. Daily he descended to thirty feet collecting conch shells and lobster. He would breathe on a hose connected to an air source on the boat above. On this day, he was on the bottom, the visibility poor, and suddenly saw a shark about ten feet away. He decided to stay still until the shark moved on. After what seemed like a long time, the shark finally left.

Feeling fine after the dive, he returned home and took a shower. He felt tingling in his legs and collapsed. He was paralyzed from the waist down. Nitrogen from the dive that collected in his tissues passed into his blood as bubbles. They stopped in his spinal cord. Since Puerto Rico did not have a dive chamber, he was transported to us via helicopter flying low. Any increase in altitude could make the diver's condition worsen.

When he arrived, he was assessed, oxygen and IV fluids initiated, a urinary catheter inserted, and wheeled into the chamber, placing him on a small cot. I sat on the opposite cot, assembling the equipment we would be using. The Navy timetable would take seven hours. I don't speak Spanish, but I had compiled a few pages of frequently used words and phrases along with medical questions. Juan and I spent the time talking with my limited communication skills. He was apprehensive about being able to walk after the treatment. The need for a catheter was also a big fear.

At the end of the treatment, he was able to wobble out of the chamber on his own, carrying the catheter bag. The next morning, he returned for a second treatment, without a catheter, and after three treatments recovered almost fully.

I had the pleasure of being involved with several interesting patients undergoing hyperbaric therapy for dive injuries. Even one that was found floating face down on the surface after a dive and required a chest tube for a collapsed lung. She recovered enough to travel home with her family by plane.

Because my home was over five hundred feet of altitude, I could not return home immediately after being at an equivocal sixty feet underwater in the chamber. I occasionally spent evenings reading in my car for a while before I could drive home.

The hyperbaric physician had forty-foot sailboat and invited us to sail. I was the galley chef as they sailed the boat. The first time we went out to sea, we motored out from the marina, finally reaching deep water. The motor was shut off and the sails hoisted. The feeling is indelible in my mind. I caught my breath as my body felt lifted. My bucket list includes owning a sailboat.

Family and friends visited us while we were in St. Thomas. My brother and his wife came to visit. Since we could see several small islands from the patio, we decided to rent a small boat, cruise around a couple of islands and snorkel. The six-passenger outboard was easy to use, and Bill was at the helm. We had two other friends join us and with lots of food and drinks, the six of us set off for an afternoon of snorkeling. We snorkeled for a while off the nearest island and set off for the next island nearby.

The boat motor coughed and died. We called the emergency number of the rental shop, and they agreed to send a boat to tow us back. Sitting back and enjoying our snacks and drinks, we realized that we were drifting in a fast current out to deep water. Forty-five minutes later, we heard a honk from our rescue boat. It took over ninety minutes to return to our original spot where we snorkeled. We nervously laughed at our adventure at dinner that night. That is, until a neighbor came over to visit and told us that the island where we had been snorkeling was known for sharks. My brother will no doubt remind me of this story for years to come.

Our life was filled with more pleasure than work until we were notified that a hurricane was headed our way. We were camping on a nearby island, lounging in hammocks on the beach. We quickly hopped on a boat going back to St. Thomas. Our plan was to spend the night sleeping on the cots in the chamber since we lived about six feet above sea level in a tiny cabana on a beach. We packed many of our things in our car and left it in the parking lot of the hospital. We had spent the day helping friends board up their houses. Many marinas were nearly empty. Boats had chosen small coves to ride out the storm. The storm never came.

The next Thursday, warnings were issued for another bad storm on Saturday with heavy rain and winds. Many people were exhausted from the last weekend and were not as cautious. Many boats did not leave the marina. We decided to stay home.

There were a group of small houses with shuttered windows on the beach area around us. Bougainvillea vines bloomed everywhere, even on our patio.

The large bar in the center of the compound had a long shiny wood bar complete with a coconut tree growing through the center. Most nights we were treated to island music while we ate food cooked in large cut off oil drums. The entire area was fine white sand, no shoes needed. It was like living at summer camp.

As Saturday progressed, the rain became heavier and as the sky turned darker, the radio predicted winds over one hundred miles per hour. We lost power. Bill began collecting blankets, bottled water, and our important papers. "We're going over to Larry's house. He said we could go there if things got bad." We grabbed pillows and quickly began running down a path to the new house being constructed. It was solid wood construction, just completed and empty. Larry had offered respite to any of us in the compound if the storm was bad.

We found the house empty except for some old mattresses and springs leaning against a wall in the living room. Bill grabbed a mattress, and we found a bathroom at the back of the house. We huddled there for hours as the storm raged outside. It sounded like coconuts hitting the roof. Cracking sounds in the roof were frightening. A wet dog ran into the bathroom followed by Larry. He was laughing. "I was in bed and looked up to see the sky. My roof was gone. Poor little Pedro beat me here."

The noises continued while we all huddled together. When the eye came over, the silence was deafening. We heard screaming as a young couple ran into the bathroom. They had been hanging onto the drain under the kitchen sink until the storm receded. She was hysterical, and soon calmed down when she realized she was safe. The eye passed, and as the storm started up again, we heard freight trains coming overhead. The water was being sucked away in the toilet. At one point, we heard a ringing bell maybe from a boat.

The storm finally passed about six in the morning. We came out as a group into a terrible scene. Yes, it was a boat bell, and the boat was sitting under the living room window.

When we saw the couple's house, we all started to laugh. The only thing on the cement slab was a toilet. Larry's house was gone. Our house had no roof, and all our belongings were soaked. Larry and Bill went down to the bar to see if they could somehow save all the frozen and refrigerated food. Bill rigged up a gas generator. They knew that looters would soon be there to steal liquor and cigarettes. They piled beer, cigarettes and other items on the porch and took turns that night guarding the premises. The couple left to stay with friends who lived a short distance away.

We had a Coleman stove and lantern, plenty of water for now and a dry place to stay. We fixed up places to sleep and gathered food. I was the chief cook. Bill used his skills and repaired a second generator. He and Larry spent days salvaging food and moving supplies. At night they patrolled.

We heard from Larry's friends that the airport was closed, part of the hospital was blown away, and there was no telephone service. There was no housework, but when I went out in the morning to sweep the porch, giant tarantulas came out by the dozens. They were sunning themselves. They're gross but not vicious. I gently swept them into the yard. It made me wonder where all the animals go in a storm like this. When I looked up to the hills on the island, there were no leaves. I was able to see homes I never saw before, and many had no roofs.

News travels fast and we heard that a National Guard unit from Boston was arriving at the hospital. When the roads were passable, Bill and I went to his trailer that was filled with auto parts. It was where he repaired cars. The trailer was empty. He was very upset that his car parts and tools had been stolen. Three cars he had fixed and rented out to friends were lost somewhere on the island. We rode by the hospital to check the damage. The military was just setting up tents. I spoke to a guardsman who told me what time to report for medical duty the next morning.

I got to play "Hot Lips" like on M.A.S.H. Several of the nurses arrived to assist patients who no longer had a doctor or hospital. Very ill patients were being airlifted by Huey helicopters landing on the front lawn of the hospital. It was exciting except for the heat. Hearing the helicopters outside was a real rush.

I approached the guardsman operating communications, but we were not allowed to call out. On day three, someone told me about a telephone at the hospital that miraculously worked. I was able to call our families and my recruiter.

Within the week, I was told that a job and apartment were ready for me in Fort Pierce, Florida. My only clothing was from a heavy bureau that survived the wind. My books were soaked. My new computer and printer were ruined, all my furniture, TV and vacuum were destroyed.

Bill decided to stay back to find his cars and help Larry with the bar and buildings. He promised to leave as soon as possible. I left him the phone number of my travel nurse recruiter. She would give him my new address in Florida.

As soon as plane tickets were available, I flew to Florida and rented a car at the airport. I probably looked like a homeless person. I had one moldy suitcase and a backpack. I had on a t-shirt, jean shorts and sandals. My new apartment was a welcome haven. Dry with running water. I took a very long shower and cried with relief. I hoped that Bill would leave St. Thomas soon and join me.

# CHAPTER 4 FLORIDA

1995

The apartment complex in Fort Pierce is lovely but feels so different from my cute beach bungalow in St. Thomas. Air conditioning doesn't compare to warm fresh breezes from the ocean. Instead of sea gulls I hear car doors closing and kids in the parking lot. There are eight lanes of city traffic all driving on the right side of the road. I'm so afraid I'll get distracted and pull out on the left by mistake.

Bill called me today after reaching my recruiter. It will take only a few more days to wind up things up in St. Thomas. I bought him some new clothes to tide him over until he can shop. I'll be glad when he's safely here.

On my first day at the emergency department, I learn that I'm working at the Fort "Fierce Gun and Knife Club". However, being in a real hospital is in sharp contrast to St. Thomas. The hospital is large and the emergency room very busy with lots of trauma. After working as a trauma nurse in Detroit in the 1970s, it's like riding a bike. In fact, I really enjoy the fast pace and exciting cases. Bill arrived two weeks after I started my new job and loves hearing all the ER stories.

I told him about an interesting case. Two teen-aged boys, cousins, shot each other over the affections of a girl they both liked. Neither had life threatening wounds.

Unknown to me, they had been placed in adjoining cubicles. I was behind the curtain cleaning the wounds of one teen when I heard a commotion. Hearing someone yelling about killing the person who shot his son, I knew my patient and I were in danger.

Instructing my young man to lie still, I covered his head and rolled him down the hall to a safe area. He grabbed my hand and said, "Thank you, nurse. You saved my life." Our security police made sure both families remained in the waiting room.

The thirteen weeks flew by. There were many fatal gunshot wounds, especially on the night shift. It was like being back in Detroit. We frequently needed to call security to collect and store guns on arriving patients. It wasn't unusual to undress a patient packing a Dirty Harry gun.

Twelve-hour shifts meant working three or four days a week. That left lots of time to check out all the local restaurants. There was a family Italian restaurant within walking distance from our apartment. The owners and their family ate their dinner at a large round table near the kitchen. We were there so often that they knew our names and it felt like we were part of the family. The food was incredible, especially their salads and eggplant parmigiana.

My next assignment was in West Palm Beach. In December 1995, we moved into a new apartment in a nice area. It had a work-out room, pool and was near the hospital. My new hospital emergency room was huge, busy, modern, and fast paced. There were many traveling nurses there. Every hospital emergency room had a personal color for scrub uniforms, and now I wear light blue. The last job was cranberry red. At this rate, I'll have a rainbow assortment of scrubs.

Large stainless steel cupboards holding equipment in the ER opened only with a patient number. Medications also need my personal code and the patient number. All the recording is computerized, down to ordering lab work and EKG's. If there is a delay in getting the patient's information quickly, they have no number, and a delay in treatment.

For multiple reasons, I found this job frustrating. I had committed to a six-month contract and couldn't wait to find another position. At least we liked the area and found lots to do here. There was a nearby delicatessen where we ate many evenings and sometimes brunch on Sunday mornings. Their pastrami sandwiches were scrumptious. We found restaurants overlooking the ocean, hung out at one of the malls or drove to nearby local attractions to help pass the time until we could leave.

One of our favorite trips was in the Everglades. We stopped at an alligator park, a nursery for baby 'gators. They ranged from a few inches to huge. Even though the big ones were behind fences, their massive jaws and rows of jagged teeth were formidable and scary. The snake exhibit had bleachers, filled with people enjoying a snake show. There were snakes of all sizes and designs. My favorite was an albino snake, about twelve inches long. When the snake expert asked for a volunteer, I raised my hand. Bill looked at me in shock. "Are you crazy?"

I never told him about my snake chasing as a child. I love snakes, provided they're not near me and venomous.

The snake handler had a large boa constrictor around his neck. Her name was Sally and the handler assured me that she was friendly. I have a picture of Sally wrapped around my neck just in case you don't believe me. Her skin was silky smooth and creepy cold. The Everglades is such a primeval park, where you can forget what century it is.

The travel nurses have a communication network. Details about the assignments are shared. Bill and I became good friends with many. One evening at dinner, we began talking about our next assignment selection. Felice, who had also been in St. Thomas with us, spoke up excitedly.

"Guess what?  I heard today that Guam is hiring nurses for their emergency room." She looked at me directly, with a big smile and raised eyebrows.

I looked at Bill. He smiled.

"Why not?" I asked him.

"Sure. Where the hell is Guam, anyway?"

"I'm not sure, but we'll look on a map later. All I know is that it's got to have some spectacular diving. I'm game."

Felice and I called our recruiters first thing in the morning. The wheels of progress were turning. I guess they really wanted two ER nurses with over thirty years of experience between them. Within two days, we were hired to start our new jobs in Agana, Guam. Felice would be going alone since her boyfriend had a full-time job in Naples, Florida. Bill and I were excited about moving again.

Packing containers is getting easier. Now we know what we'll need and what we don't want to buy. Neither of us knows anything about Guam. We're off to the library for information.

The post office in Guam was difficult to contact. The postmaster was not entirely happy about my thirty containers that would sit in his post office until I arrived. This time, we had more clothing, linens, books, tools, and small kitchen items. I even packed a small vacuum, a computer and printer, new non-breakable dishes and glasses and our diving equipment. We'll be gone for at least a year, maybe longer?

Getting a passport for Bill was next on the list. We would certainly need current passports since we were staying overnight in Kyoto, Japan on the way to Guam. We were both very excited about the trip.

I have signed a one-year contract with the travel nurse agency. My family and friends now groan when I call and tell them I'm moving on. They have a long list of prior addresses penciled into their address books. This time, I'm traveling halfway across the globe.

# CHAPTER 5
# COSTA RICA



While enjoying the island life in St. Thomas, Bill and I had discussed retiring someday in a warm climate with sandy beaches and waving palm trees. Now that we were living in Florida and I had time between assignments, it was the perfect time to start looking for the ideal retirement location. I collected books on many islands but the one that most interested us was Costa Rica. It had a stable democratic government and good medical care. Real estate was inexpensive. Many American expats lived there comfortably on retirement incomes.

Armed with a Spanish dictionary, we were off on a two-week trip. We planned our trip to include two days in Puerto Rico, then off to Costa Rica for the remainder of our vacation.

The flight from St. Thomas to Puerto Rico was short. We arrived at the capital, San Juan, just after eleven in the morning. This gave us the day to explore. We were interested in visiting the historic fort there, Castillo San Cristobel. Using brochures from the hotel lobby, we found the fort easily. We left a modern city and stepped into history. The fort sits along the shore, built in the 1700s for protection from land and sea intruders. If only the weathered stones could tell tales of pirates and battles.

Bill and I ambled along the long walkways of the ramparts, high above the Caribbean Sea. Smooth rolling waves with white caps rhythmically exploded on the fort, sending a fine mist from its crystal green waters. American flags waving in the sea breeze, reminded us that Puerto Rico is a commonwealth of the United States. The labyrinth of rooms inside the fort smelled musty as we weaved our way through the many floors of the castle.

Wanting to see as much as possible, we walked back to our hotel to change for the evening. The Bomberia Restaurant brochure appealed to us, and we were not disappointed. We sat on the deck overlooking the ocean enjoying a fresh fish special. The magenta sunset completed the scene. The meal and the fine wine were relaxing. We would be off to our next destination, Costa Rica, tomorrow afternoon.

In the morning, I asked Bill, "Do you want to stop by a pharmacy so I can get more film? I saw one nearby. Maybe we can catch a bus downtown to find a breakfast restaurant?

"Sure. That sounds good. I'll be ready in a jiffy."

As we exited the pharmacy, we crossed the street to the bus stop. We had been there only a few minutes when a car pulled up and rolled down the window. A pleasant man said, "The bus is not in service on the weekends. If you are looking for a breakfast place, I can drop you off at my favorite."

I glanced at Bill, and he nodded. I told the man, "Sure, that would be nice. Thank you."

As the car pulled away, the gentleman told us that he made breakfast for his wife on Sunday and was on his way to the market. He added that he was the lieutenant governor of Puerto Rico and chatted pleasantly all the way to his favorite breakfast restaurant. Thanking him and waving as he left, I turned to Bill and said, "Can you believe that? This should be a terrific trip if this is how it starts." He certainly chose well for us. The mounds of fresh fruit, choices of entrees and freshly brewed coffee started our day perfectly.

Our flight in the early afternoon to Costa Rica was short.

Flying into the Juan Santamaria International Airport, we saw the city below, smothered by a layer of smog. It was apparent that there are no emission controls. The airport was modern and easy to navigate to the luggage area. Taxis were lined up at the arrival gate. We had reservations at the Hotel Don Carlos. As I attempted to converse in Spanish with the taxi driver, he was nodding and smiling. I guess he understood as he took us right to our hotel.

The hotel was amazing. Tiled floors, bamboo furniture and potted palms made the lobby so tropical and inviting. The staff spoke English! On the way to our room, we walked through a stone patio with colorful plants.  I caught a glimpse of an elegant dining room with white tablecloths and crystal glasses sparkling in the sunshine.

Our hotel room was as large as a suite. Since this is coffee country, the coffee maker on the counter will be enjoyed. Outside the shuttered window was a tall tree with graceful branches that ended with bright red flowers in full bloom. Looking closely between the branches, I saw flashing reds and greens of parrots, squawking loudly, each in their own key. Do parrots sleep at night?

Turning to Bill, I suggested, "How about a tropical drink and then gather some brochures from the lobby? "

True to his nature, Bill smiled and nodded in assent.

The bartender made us a milky drink with crushed ice, coconut and pineapple. Bill gave him a thumbs up as we left and we said, "*Gracias.*" The desk clerk told us it was a short walk to a park with shops and restaurants. I selected some brochures to look at later and slid them into the large purse I always carry while on trips.

This area of the city was quiet and without the smog. Walking felt good after a long plane trip. The park was a topiary, an ornamental garden of sculpted trees and bushes. An elephant true to size was the first trimmed bush to catch my eye. Rows of animal shaped bushes took up acres of the park. A man on a ladder was trimming overhead branches that formed a tunnel.

Barrels of colorful flowers in front of a restaurant make it easy to decide where to eat lunch. The owner greeted us in Spanish, and I replied, *"buenos tardes"* as I accepted a menu. I looked at Bill. "The menu is in Spanish."

Bill suggested," Now would be a good time to get out your dictionary. All the menus will be in Spanish. We'd better learn some basic words if we're going to be here two weeks."

"Good idea. I see *pan*, that means bread and *sopa*, that's soup. I think it has vegetables in it. Want to try it?"

Bill pointed to our selection in the menu for the waitress. She asked us what we wanted to drink. I know *agua*, so I held up two fingers and said *"Agua, por favor."* I would like ice, but I don't know how to say it. I'll have to do some studying tonight.

We agreed this was best soup we've ever had. Fresh bread on the bottom of a large bowl, topped with a tomato-based sauce and vegetables. I copied the name down on my Spanish terms cheat sheet.

Completing checking out of our hotel in the morning, the desk clerk called a car rental for us. We both felt rested today so I guess parrots must sleep at night.

We quickly found our route, thankful that they drive on the right side of the road. Bill was driving and I was navigating. I had a list of street signs in English and Spanish. We're on our way to Lake Arenal, about three hours north of the capital.

As we drove through the countryside, we were taken by the breathtaking beauty of this country. We can see coffee fields precariously planted on hillsides, neat squares of land fenced by trees, planted for fences. As we approached the lake, we could see Lake Arenal's active volcano. It's thin trail of smoke from the volcano visible miles away.

Our hotel, basic as a Motel 6, had a view of the volcano. After checking in we decided to ride around the lake. Many US citizens purchase inexpensive property in this area. Large homes are seen far from the road, with barbed wire fences on the property. It is a law in Costa Rica that if you are not living on the land, settlers can assume ownership.

One of our brochures showed a spa at the volcano base. We found the spa and after changing into our bathing suits in a small cabana, we walked to the riverbed of black volcanic stones. Lying down among the stones and shallow stream of moderately hot water, we lounged in its soothing warmth.

The next evening, we were booked on a bus trip to the volcano. The volcano activity is best seen at night. We stood in a field, mesmerized by nature's Disney like fireworks. I asked myself, if this volcano is so active, do I want to be this close? We will be off tomorrow to take the ferry across the west coast at Puntarenas. We'll spend a day or two sightseeing there.

There was a four hour wait until the ferry boarded. Bill and I found a restaurant to have a relaxing lunch. That day I was wearing a Myrtle Beach t-shirt. A lady with a small infant approached us, asking if we were American. She told us she was from New Jersey, married a local man, and happy to meet someone from home. She and her husband own this restaurant and have a home nearby. She insisted we visit her home until the ferry left.

As we approached the edge of her property, armed guards were at the entrance of their estate. She explained that many locals have guards. I began having second thoughts about living here.

We spent the remainder of the day touring the Pacific coast of Costa Rica. I have never been to the California coast, but I imagine that it looks similar. Taking the bridge back to the main part of Costa Rica, we were off to the jungle in Tortuguero, near Nicaragua on the Caribbean coast. There is a recurring road sign that I couldn't find in my notes.

We enjoyed many conversations with locals. We asked about the sign and what it meant. It was a "one way" sign. How many times did we go the wrong way? Thank goodness the roads didn't have much traffic.

A local told us that tourists disappear and are warned not to venture into Panama, even along the border. We kept that in mind traveling to our destination. I followed the map carefully. My Spanish is improving but I still get lots of smiles and nods. Many people ask me how to say the word in English. One restaurant owner tried to give me his cute chihuahua. That conversation in Spanish was confusing and I was relieved when we left without a dog.

Staying at a local hotel, a bus picked us up for a "must do" if you're in Costa Rica. River boats holding six people loaded us at the dock. There was a couple on our boat from South Dakota who were avid birdwatchers. We traveled up the narrow Tortuguero Canals, our guide pointing out the vast array of wildlife. We saw turtles, monkeys, crocodiles, birds, and butterflies. We smiled as our two birdwatchers excitedly pointed out birds and wrote in their books. They told us their bird log dated back thirty years.

Our destination was a village called Parismina. It took our river boats four hours to reach our destination. The entire village was one narrow dirt road and a few houses. The litter was reflective of its forlorn nature. A larger building housed the general store and restaurant.

The cabins were clean and comfortable. Our first meal was an awakening for me. I do not eat beans or rice. They were served at each meal. Other than a few vegetables, I drank the local beer and ate all dessert served.

Each day we were taken by boat along narrow canals

through the jungle. White faced monkeys screeched at us from the trees. Crocodiles slithered into the water alongside the boat. I think if I had seen a tree snake hanging over the water, it would have been all over. Our guide, Eddy, was informative. We saw a variety of birds and our bird experts named them all. Bill and I politely smiled then rolled our eyes behind their backs.

This village is located on the Caribbean Sea. Black sand lined the deserted beach. Bill and I walked a short way hearing loud splashes offshore. Blue marlins are caught here and can weigh over 1000 pounds. When they breech the water, they land with a sound like thunder. Maybe that's marlin we hear.

At dinner we asked our guide why nobody was on the beach. We were told nobody swam there due to sharks.

Bill read about marlin fishing here. The guide offered to take him out the next morning for two hundred dollars an hour. He was so excited to catch a big one and get a picture for his family and friends at home.

At dawn, a gentle rap at the door and Bill was off on his big adventure. Hours later, he returned and walked up to the cabin slowly. From behind his back, he raised his arm. A six-inch fish hung limply from a fishing line. I took a picture and we laughed about it for weeks. He did have an exciting ocean trip with the fisherman. He bragged about the ones he almost caught.

The last two days of our vacation we spent in the mountains above the city of San Jose. The resort was quiet, except for the parrots, and had a large pool. We enjoyed down time, reading, and relaxing by the pool. Occasionally I would point out a bird and say, "Hey Bill. There goes a red headed flea flicker!" We would break out in gales of laughter.

We spent one morning at the city market. The stench was overwhelming. Dead ducks and chickens hung from wires. Large trays of every type of fish attracted flies. The entire city block had vendors of not only food but clothing and household supplies. No big stores like Walmart here.

While downtown, I stopped at an urgent care clinic. The doctor on duty had no patients so we talked for about an hour. I asked questions about working in the medical field in Costa Rica. I found out that I would have to take my nursing boards in Spanish.  About all I could say in Spanish is *bano (bathroom)* and *cervesa fria* (a cold beer). We would have to learn to speak Spanish if we lived here.

Our flight back through Puerto Rico to St. Thomas Sunday morning was uneventful. We stayed overnight in a two-star motel near the airport. The room smelled musty and the noise from the next room loud. We got up so early that we caught an early flight back to St. Thomas. The islands were a welcome sight. When we opened the door to our apartment, the fresh breeze from the ocean welcomed us home.

# CHAPTER 6 GUAM

1996

When Felice, my traveling nurse friend who worked with me in Florida, told me that Guam was looking for ER nurses, it was a no brainer. Bill and I agreed that living on a tiny island in the South Pacific was tempting.

The island of Guam is a tiny speck on any map, hundreds of miles of open ocean in any direction. I saw myself swinging in a hammock between two palm trees, a machete topped coconut in my hand.

Our flight from Miami was fourteen hours to Narita, Japan. I was ecstatic that this trip included an overnight in Japan. We left on July third and arrived at Tokyo International Narita Airport on July fourth.

It was early evening with some sunlight left, allowing us to see the flat expanses of countryside with squares of rice fields from the bus window. As we neared the hotel, I was disappointed that we would not be going through Narita. As we hauled our luggage into the hotel, we were impressed by the open, modern lobby. The desk staff were welcoming and spoke English. Our tenth-floor room offered a view of a salmon sunset over the countryside as peaceful as the night's sleep I was anticipating.

Starving, we sought out the restaurant. The menu was varied, catering to international travelers. We ordered a local fish tempura with fresh vegetables. Delicious. For dessert, I ordered tiramisu. Bill ordered green tea ice cream called Matcha.

We shared our perfect choices. By the end of the meal, we agreed that we were exhausted. A good night's sleep would give us energy for moving into our Guam apartment tomorrow.

Sinking into the soft luxurious bed relaxed us into a deep sleep. I don't think I even wrinkled the sheets. After an omelet, toast, and coffee, we joined our group back to the airport by bus for our five-hour flight to Guam.

The Tokyo airport was bustling with travelers, each hastily seeking their gate. I stopped to buy postcards, candy, and T-shirts for my grandchildren. After we picked up a snack and a cold drink, we found our gate.  I took out an Agatha Christie novel but couldn't concentrate on anything but making mental to do lists.

Blue was all we saw from the plane window. Ocean as far as the eye could see. Sometimes I would see a white streak in the water, hoping it was a whale or shark, but would realize that it was a random wave. No boats. No islands. Just an enormous expanse of blue water.

Suddenly, we saw Guam's green coated mountains, the apron of reef surrounding the island and then felt the bump of the landing gear. Guam is like a mushroom. The island is hilly, gradually flattening to a beach or water. A person can walk out in the knee-deep water for over one hundred feet, and then THE ABYSS.

We landed in Agana, Guam. From the taxi to our apartment, we noted that the countryside had small homes, nestled into hills. On our way through the main part of town we saw large hotels along the beach, and high-end expensive stores in the area. The taxi driver told us that the Koreans who vacationed in Guam owned the hotel and stores. The residents patronized locally owned stores.

It was a short ride to our apartment. Our new home was on the second floor of a multi apartment building. It was furnished with a couch and a couple of rattan chairs. The one bedroom had a double bed and dresser. The kitchen had a stove and refrigerator, and a few dishes in the cupboards. Thankfully, our cartons contained necessities.

I asked Bill, "How about we find the post office and see if our cartons are there? We can check out the town and find the hospital. Thank goodness I have a couple of days before I start work. I hope that Felice gets here soon. I think she's coming in tomorrow. Maybe we can find the car rental place first. That would save us some taxi expense."

Patiently, he smiled and took a deep breath. "Yes, to all the above. "I saw a car rental in town not far from here. Why don't we walk downtown? I don't know about you, but I could use some exercise after sitting so long. Maybe we can find a restaurant for dinner."

Three blocks from our apartment, we found the main part of town with a few small stores, and across the street, a wide beach with a few sunbathers. There was an open Enterprise car rental. Choices of cars were limited but we found a compact car.

As we left with our rental Bill said, "I can find a junker somewhere and fix it up, so we'll have a car while we're here. We can sell it when we leave."

"Sounds like a plan. It's sure nice to have a handy man around the house."

All I got for a reply was a sideways grin.

The post office and city buildings looked like any other town. In studying Guam, I learned that the indigenous people here are Chamorro, primarily Catholic and have a rich cultural blend of old ways and new.

We found our cartons at the post office but had to make three trips. The man in the post office was friendly but looked relieved when we carried off the cartons from his small holding area.

Having worked up an appetite, we found a restaurant nestled in palm trees along the beach. We both fell in love with Vietnamese food.

The owner, a child sized woman, sent all six of her siblings from Vietnam to the U.S. for their education. She was the last to leave and supports her husband and two children with her restaurant. Her egg rolls are so popular that she stays up late at night making hundreds to serve in the restaurant and for take-out. Her two elementary school children seat the patrons, take orders, serve, and collect payment. We became a part of their family, eating there three to four times a week while the kids did their homework at a back table.

Felice arrived. All she carried was a knapsack and a small suitcase. She had one plate, and one set of silverware. Apparently, she expected us to take her to work and supply items that she didn't bring. We found that she ate soup for most meals and wondered if maybe she had no money. As time passed, we realized that this was how she preferred to live. Eventually she bought a bicycle for days that we weren't on the same shift.

The first day at work, Felice and I were taken on a tour. When we reached the ER, two female U.S. doctors stood up and shook our hands. "Thank goodness. Our first two American nurses." Felice and I were used to ordering labs, performing procedures, starting IVs, ordering x-rays, and presenting the information to the ER doc. When it was busy, it saved time. We had experience and had been trained to perform these duties. The hospital was small, limited in their scope of surgeries and specialties such as pediatrics. I was relieved that this hospital seemed much better than the one in St. Thomas.

I loved my job at the hospital and the ER staff was welcoming. Felice and I felt like accepted members of a team. Bill found a 1989 rusted red Ford, without an engine. Making friends with mechanics at a local garage, he bought an engine and soon we had a good car. No rental fees. Our apartment was now a cozy home. We were settling into our new life here in Guam.

About a month after we arrived, we sought out a local dive shop. Buying dive equipment was pricey. Keeping safety in mind, we bought good equipment and joined the local dive club. The club had many members and offered classes and trips. Diving in the South Pacific is why we came here.

Life goes on even on small islands. Our friendly ER docs and a female chiropractor invited me to join them at a Mary Kay demonstration. The hotel on the ocean was high end, had four pools, two restaurants, and palm trees in abundance. After working with these two women in the ER, I suspected that they were unpredictable. Their friend was quiet but seemed nice. As we entered the demonstration, we sat down in a filled room as the event began.

In less than five minutes, one of the ER docs stood up and headed for the door. We all followed like baby ducklings. She stopped at the edge of a pool in a quiet area of the hotel. She pulled her dress over her head, and dove into the pool. The second ER doc did the same. The two of us left just looked at each other, smiled, shrugged our shoulders, pulled off our clothes, and joined the others. In our underwear, we laughed and enjoyed the balmy water. I had never in my life stripped and jumped into a public pool. Thank goodness I had worn a new matched set of bra and panties. It was dark and we were isolated. For a while. We noticed that a crowd was gathering in our vicinity. Not wanting the headlines of tomorrow's paper, we slipped back into our dresses and made our way out. I never told Bill.

We attended an open house at the Air Force base on the north end of the island. I stood at the rear opening of a huge plane that transported trucks. I couldn't believe this plane could get off the ground when fully loaded. I had no idea that there was a large American presence in Guam.

The palm trees in Guam have a fruit that attracts bats. Bat brains are a local delicacy causing the supply of bats to be depleted on most of the island. There is a disease only in Guam, like Alzheimer's disease, related to eating bat brains. I'm not even tempted.

Bill met one of the Navy guys while working on our car. He invited us to visit him and his wife on the Navy base at the south end of the island. They were from Florida and had been there two years with their three dogs. Ben and Sherry were what I would call a power couple. He was an attorney, and she was a charismatic hostess who wrote for the base newspaper. We became good friends immediately. They treated us to a cookout of hamburgers and a menu of back home food in their back yard. Over drinks, we talked well into the night about family and travels.

Sherry loved to snorkel and invited Felice, Bill, and I to join her at a beach on the base that was accessible only by climbing down a cliff.  And yes, we did have to shimmy down a narrow trail and along a cliff edge to reach the beach. It was worth it. The corals and fish were even better than in St. Thomas. We found starfish that were neon blue. We would take advantage of that spot many times while in Guam.

The Filipino families frequently celebrated religious feasts. We were invited to family dinners and were amazed at the amount of food. I learned to love pancit, a tasty noodle dish. Thank goodness they always had leftovers for me to take home.

One of the girls from the ER invited us to her home for a birthday party. She offered us a drink of tuba. Bill does not usually drink alcohol, but politely asked, "What is tuba?" We had seen signs along the roads, TUBA FOR SALE. The first time I saw the sign, I thought some high school kid was selling his band instrument. The second and third time, I figured it was not that kind of tuba. We learned that tuba is a popular drink of fermented coconut milk. Bill took a polite sip, but I liked it.

We were active members of the dive club and signed up for a trip to Saipan. The island was north of Guam, a short trip by plane. We would be there for the weekend, to check out the island and take a special dive in a cavern. We joined two couples and rented a car. Our driver was local and comfortable driving on the left. Saipan is primarily Japanese with most of the homes reflecting an Oriental design.

Today was a "grotto" dive. We entered the cave after a long walk down narrow stone steps. The air tanks were available at the cave entrance. Each diver would connect a tank to their gear, then proceed into the cave. The rock footing was uneven and sharp. As we waited in line for our turn to jump in, the light was dim, making me more anxious. Bill let me lean on him while I put on my flippers. I jumped into the murky water, gave the ok sign, and descended, waiting for him to join me. We joined the group underwater, and when we reached forty feet, the dive master pointed up. Above us was a hole in the ocean floor. Sunlight shot rays of light into the water below. It was like swimming in a fishbowl. We followed the light and emerged to warm water of the ocean floor above.

Our dive group enjoyed our tour of the coral reef with large green turtles whose mosaic shells were works of art. There were schools of barracuda and tuna, and scary white tipped reef sharks in the distance. They couldn't be too far away for me. I still remember the movie, *JAWS*. Our time underwater went too fast, and we ascended to our boat and sunshine. What an amazing dive to add to my log.

A few weeks after we returned home, we signed up for a night dive. We purchased the necessary underwater lights, and that next evening we joined the group receiving instructions from the dive master. We were across the street from our dive shop and had practiced dives here many times. However, being underwater at thirty feet in inky darkness is eerie. The only light is in your hand. Amazing what critters you can see only at night. Tiny shrimps were sparkling pink. Reflective eyes were everywhere. We hovered around a huge piece of coral, shining our light into crevices to uncover night creatures. It was fun and scary. I prefer being underwater in the daytime.

Since I have so much trouble with buoyancy, I took advantage of a "zen" buoyancy class. Hula hoops were floating at various levels. The practice was to get through the hula hoop without hitting the tank on your back. Not easy. The other skill was to sit on the ocean floor, rise, and sit down with inhaling and exhaling without losing balance. The next time I went diving, I felt more in control.

When we had a free afternoon, we would scuba dive near the dive shop. The depth of the ocean there was about thirty feet and level. A good place to just relax and check out some reef fish. However, I had a stalker there. I could see a thin silver fish out of the corner of my eye. It was always at the same distance, waiting, watching. It was a barracuda someone told me. All I could think of was all those lethal needle teeth.

My one-year contract was coming to an end. We didn't want to leave. One of the ER docs asked me if I planned to stay on the island. Her friend ran an urgent care clinic and needed a PA. After fifteen years as an RN, I had attended Physician Assistant school in 1974, in Hershey, Penn. Travel nursing contracts were more common, so I had not been working as a physician assistant.

I interviewed for the urgent care position and was hired. We were staying! That meant more diving and traveling. We decided that we would look for a house. There were lots of military families coming and going so furniture was available. Felice had accepted a job on a cruise ship.

Driving around the town of Maite, a rural section of the island, we found a small white adobe house on a corner lot that had a rental sign in the yard. Bill pulled into the driveway. As we walked around the house, a short balding man with a German

Shepherd approached us from across the street. The man smiled and said, "It seems that my dog, Sargent, likes you. Are you interested in renting my house?"

Bill shook his hand and we introduced ourselves. He told us his name was Norman and his family owned all the houses along the street. As we walked through the house, it just felt right. Although a thorough cleaning was needed, we would have plenty of room and a large yard. We accepted the terms of the rental and gave him a down payment. He and Bill got talking about cars and an hour later, we left after agreeing we could move in anytime.

Since I was on the day shift, Bill was free to go to the house the next morning and begin cleaning out debris left by prior tenants. During that week we cleaned the appliances, painted the kitchen cabinets bright yellow, repaired the screens, and found furniture at the Navy base garage sale on the weekend. Bill gave the outside of the house a fresh coat of paint. We needed to purchase an air conditioner as Guam temperatures during the day can be over 100 and during the night, the humidity is so oppressive it feels solid. At the end of a week, we had a new home. The property was so improved that the neighbors asked Norman who bought his house.

That first weekend, we had time to explore. The beach was a five-minute walk through the cemetery across the street. The ocean was dark blue with large scraggly rocks along the shore. The beach was flat, long, and deserted. Low bushes and scattered rocks joined the sand for as far as we could see. Since we were this close to the ocean, we enjoyed an onshore breeze even on hot days.

We took daily walks on our nearby beach, noticing that there were no birds in the trees anywhere on the island. We saw a few terns on the beach only. Norman told us to watch for brown tree snakes. They came out at night and sometimes are found inside a house in plants. They have eaten all the birds on the island and have no natural predators. The wheel wells of planes leaving the island are checked carefully for hitchhiker snakes. I made sure our screen door was closed tight.

There was a dog population problem in Guam. Thousands roam wild. There were many weird looking inbred dogs all running wild, and sadly hit by passing cars. Locals tied them outside their homes but didn't treat them as pets. We bought large bags of dog food and fed many in our back yard.

One morning as we walked along the beach, Bill saw a dead dog in a plastic bag in the bushes. We were horrified. Walking a short distance further, we saw a puppy, sitting on the sand, like it was waiting for us. It was a few weeks old, with black hair full of sand and bugs. I picked it up and held it in my T-shirt. I asked Bill, "Please look around to see if more puppies were left."

"I found another one under this bush. That's the only one I could find." Bill held up another puppy that could not hold up its head.

After a trip to the vet with two German Shepherd mix puppies, dehydrated, full of fleas, they were now ours. Once nursed back to health, they were the cutest, smartest dogs ever owned by humans. Like we needed two dogs to carry around the world. At this point, we could never part with them. We suspected who the father was…Norman's pure-bred German Shepherd.

Wherever Bill traveled in his truck, the puppies were in the back. My grandchildren named them Sassy and Dutchess. As they grew, they hung over the side of the truck, ears flying in the wind and tongues hanging out. They wore a perpetual dog smile.

Our nurse friends from St. Thomas invited us to California to visit them, but I always refused as I'm afraid of earthquakes. Watching earthquake horror movies on TV didn't help. I never expected to be in an earthquake in Guam, but it happened while we were at the movies. The floor under the seats began moving. In an instant, we were outside the theater. It lasted less than a minute, but the whole time I was waiting for the earth to open.

A month later, we were in our yard, talking with Norman and the ground began shaking. It lasted so long that we didn't dare move. Then the up-down movements became like someone was pulling the rug from underneath us. The ground didn't open but I thought it would at any moment. Until we left Guam, the fear of another earthquake hovered in the back of my mind.

One night while Bill watched the news, I was finishing the supper dishes. I pulled out the silverware drawer and yelled, "Bill. There's a snake in the silverware drawer! When he opened it again, it was gone but found it in with the pots and pans. As he pointed the broom handle at the snake, it wound around the broom and became airborne when he opened the door. We're told their venom would not kill an adult. Not very reassuring.

We did adopt another dog who dragged herself down our road one morning. Her teats were so big that they touched the ground. "Oh, Bill. Look at this poor yellow dog. She looks like she just had babies."

"No, Jeanne. We're not keeping that pathetic looking animal."

I made her comfy on a blanket on the porch and fed her. The girls loved her. "Let's see if we can find out who she belongs to."

Old Yeller loved living with our family. Of course, nobody claimed her. During that time, we were beginning to discuss leaving Guam. I was busy with a full-time job and no vacation time for dive trips. We sat down to talk about options. My first suggestion was Hawaii. It took only a few seconds to agree. I bought a Frommer's travel book and after checking out the towns on the big island of Hawaii, we selected Honokaa on the Hamakua coast near Hilo.

Now the preparations. No animals were allowed into Hawaii before spending a thirty-day quarantine on Oahu. There was no rabies in Hawaii. It was complicated to arrange lab work, getting in touch with the quarantine center, etc.

Our friend, Andrea, approached us about renting our house with everything in it for $1000. With Norman's permission, we accepted, and would be taking only our clothing. And as part of the deal, Old Yeller came with the house.

I arranged for an ER position in Hilo, got cages for the girls, got our tickets, mailed ahead some containers to the post office, and we were off on a new adventure. This time we had two companions. We would miss Guam but were looking forward to spending time in one of the most beautiful places on the planet.

We shipped the girls in their crates to their destination in quarantine on Oahu. The trip would take them twenty-four hours. We left on our flight, arriving in Hilo the day before Thanksgiving in 1997. The girls arrived safely at the quarantine center. Although they had thick blankets in their cages, their favorite toys, and frozen water that would thaw gradually to keep them hydrated, it was a long trip for them.

Andrea called us two weeks after we arrived in Hawaii. Old Yeller had five puppies in her closet. She insisted that we knew about the puppies. She wouldn't believe that we were shocked. She laughed and told us they were so cute, her friends at the hospital had adopted all of them.

We found our lovely hotel in Hilo where we had booked a room for a few days. Thanksgiving Day, we found Honokaa. We loved the lush postcard town but decided to live in Hilo where I would be working. In two weeks, we flew to Oahu to see the girls and in four weeks, they returned home with us. We promised the girls we would remain here a long time.

# CHAPTER 7 PALAU, ROTA AND YAP

1997

We stayed in the Pacific Islands to take advantage of the best diving spots in the world. The brochures of Palau show islands scattered in clear green water. Their limestone pedestals are worn away by the seawater leaving an apron just above the water line. Bright green vegetation grows right to the edges giving each island the look of giant green mushrooms. I was drawn to this paradise. If you wonder where Palau is located, just leave Guam and head south for hundreds of miles across open ocean. To your right are the Philippines. If you overshoot Palau, you would be in Indonesia.

Palau has the reputation for being the Mount Everest of diving. Yap is famous for their manta ray dives and stone money. Rota has incredible reef dives and hiking trips into the caves occupied by the Japanese in WWII.

Our dive shop in Guam serviced our dive equipment for safety. I didn't want to miss a single fish, so I had the shop glue on nickel sized circles of magnification inside my goggles. I need glasses but I can't wear them under my goggles.

We needed a lightweight elastic rope with a hook on the end. Dives in the Palau Islands are drift dives. The current is so strong that it pulls you along so you can't stop and enjoy the view. The hook is for latching to a piece of coral and floating at the end of a bungee cord.

Our dive equipment required a large duffel bag for each of us. Warm temperatures meant we needed only bathing suits, sandals, shorts, and T-shirts that fit in our backpacks. I used a red pen to cross out the days on our calendar. Loading the truck that last morning, we were like kids going on our first airplane ride.

I was impatient and had butterflies. The Palau airport terminal was a wooden building the size of a large garage, looking so forlorn. Our plane landed near the terminal, and on the walk across the tarmac, I felt the tropical warmth and ocean breeze. Bill and I joined the dive group, all excitedly chattering about our first dive tomorrow.

We enjoyed murals and exhibits of island life. Miniature thatched houses, carved wooden animals, colorful grass skirts and stone money are displayed along the wall. Unusual and awesome, I could have visited there for hours, but the bus was waiting.

The houses here look like one-story miniature Swiss chalets with painted decorative flowers and have metal or colorful tile roofs. The population is about 15,000. I recall being told by co-workers in Hawaii that Palau is a democratic, progressive island. Children are sent away for education and return to become the island's professionals. They also have good medical care.

The center of town reminded me of the fifties in the U.S. Sidewalks are busy with shoppers, some taking a break on colorful wooden benches. Local stores have racks of items on display. No chain stores here. I can see and hear the ocean in the distance. Restaurants line the shore.

Our motel in the downtown area is near the beach. Our room is clean and small with one double bed dresser and a tiny bathroom. We'll be reminded just how small the bathroom is when our drying bathing suits and dive equipment take up the entire space. After our dive group gets settled, we all met at the front desk to collect our dive schedules for the week.

"Bill, I'm starved. Let's go exploring and find a place to eat dinner."

"I'm hungry and thirsty. I guess we should start hydrating for our dives tomorrow. Can you put the sunscreen in your purse? I can already feel how hot the sun is here."

A couple joined us to find a restaurant. They were from New York, a banker and a teacher. Like us, they are not expert divers and it's their first trip to Palau. Tourist restaurants on the water are easy to find. A red blinking sign for "Happy Hour" captured our attention. After a couple of drinks, good conversation and local fish platter, we were full and winding down after a long day. We agreed to meet at the dive shop for a group meeting at eight in the morning.

As we were unpacking, Bill said, "You know Jeanne, there are a lot of sharks in Palau. What will you do if one comes too close?"

"You know I'm petrified of sharks. After I saw Jaws, I absolutely know that the most terrifying thing in the world is to be eaten by a shark. I've never heard of a shark eating a diver, have you?" I felt myself breaking out in a cold sweat just talking about sharks.

"No, I haven't. I'll make sure that I'm always in front of you when we're diving around sharks. The brochure said that they don't bother the divers. If I know you, you'll be too busy enjoying the fish and coral reef." Bill gave me the "make Jeanne happy" smile.

With all the hydrating and only a double bed, we were up frequently during the night. At six, I took a shower and woke Bill. "Let's have breakfast and head over to the dive shop. Maybe our friends are there early, too."

He moaned and rolled over, mumbling something about a

king size bed. I went out to get us two coffees to go.

There was an air of excitement and anticipation as we sat at the dive shop meeting site. I estimated thirty divers this week of a wide range of ages. Some looked like experts tanned and physically fit. Others, like us, needed plenty of sunscreen. Our friends, Troy and Donna saved our seats. Donna and I were so excited we could not stop chatting. The guys turned and gave us a "look" when the meeting began.

The meeting was professional, which was reassuring to me as a novice diver. We were assured that our dives would be in small groups with expert dive masters. Drawing on the giant chalkboard, he outlined the week and dives. Daily, before each dive, the groups would meet and the dive outlined. Dive safety was reviewed. Equipment repairs could be performed here at the dive shop. We visited the dive shop and what a treasure of dive equipment. I loved their T-shirts and knew I would be going home with a full suitcase.

Our first dive day I had a big choice: what bathing suit to wear? Two dive boats were bobbing at the wharf as Bill and I along with Troy and Donna boarded our boat with all our equipment. We already had our dive suits on, unzipped to the waist (trying to look cool like everyone else). Our boat took off and the adventure began. The ocean spray and the noisy engine added to the excitement.

It took about twenty minutes to reach our first dive site. There were two boats, and it took about a half hour for everyone to put on their equipment, get their tanks attached, masks on and flippers in hand. We're in the water! Bill helped me get myself together on the surface and patiently descended with me, watching to make sure I was comfortable. Soon, we were at forty feet, all the divers paired off with a buddy. Following our designated dive master, we found the appointed reef at sixty feet and large coral rock. The dive masters assisted us in attaching our bungee cords.

I drifted like bait on a hook in the current, my bungee cord tying me to the coral like an umbilical cord. Thousands of fish ignored us as they surrounded our group. It was like being invisible inside an aquarium.

Our dive master took center stage. He took out a piece of Vienna sausage and raised it above his head. Suddenly, a large blue striped fish whipped by and snatched the sausage from his hand. It was a Napoleon wrasse, about fifty pounds and its face was a caricature of a human with buggy eyes and Angelina Jolie lips. I got the feeling that this fish was part of our entertainment as he swung by again out of nowhere. All we saw were remnants of sausage floating as he darted back into the deep. I began thinking that sharks may be part of the entertainment. I crossed my arms and tried to look unappetizing.

On the way to our first dive site on the boat, Bill told me that sharks were attracted to pink. I had pink stripes on the legs of my dive suit, pink flippers, and hot pink gloves. I was at sixty feet and wondering if he was kidding.

As schools of barracuda and tuna glided by, I noticed several sharks in the distance. I tapped Bill on his shoulder and pointed. He made a circle with his hands and pointed all around us. I did a quick 360.

Sharks were everywhere. I felt like Custer. I knew my eyes must have gotten more magnified in my goggles. Bill pointed to my pink gloves. I quickly shoved my hands under my armpits. Maybe the sharks were picking which one of us they want for breakfast. I could see Bill's chest moving like he's laughing, even with the regulator in his mouth. He's going to be sorry. I took off my gloves and shoved them into the top of my bathing suit. Just in case. At least it makes my bust look bigger.

As we detached our cords, we began to drift with the current. I failed the compass class, so I relied on Bill. We were also in a large group and that relieved my stress. If I could only describe the traffic of fish here. It was like standing on a corner of a busy city street, watching a variety of people walking by. There were small colorful clown fish and huge sharks. As we became more comfortable, we ventured apart from the group. He pointed down. Way below us was a mammoth fish, bigger than a whale, with tiger like markings. It was just hanging there, not moving. Just in case it decided to come upwards, we moved on. At the end of our dive, the dive master asked everyone about their most interesting fish. We described our fish we saw below us at sixty feet. He guessed it was a tiger shark or some type of whale at eighty to one hundred feet below us.

At the end of our first day, we stopped by the dive shop for a book on local fish. After our trip in Costa Rica with the avid bird watchers, we would now be fish watchers.

Two dives a day meant that we ate a quick lunch and then dinner after the afternoon dive. We literally fell into bed at night. One day we devoted to kayaking and snorkeling. We were taken to a group of islands, where we selected our kayaks. Guides took us to freshwater lakes inside the "mushrooms". We paddled through limestone caves. We jumped from cliffs into the clear water. I searched for a rare colorful fish I had seen in my fish book. I snorkeled so long on top of the shallow reef looking for the elusive fish, I had sunburn on my back.

We swam in a freshwater lake with non-stinging jellyfish. Leaving the boat on shore, we hiked inland across mud, rocks, heavy brush, to find our lake. Wading into the lake, I could feel "things" sliding by my arms and legs. It was like swimming in alphabet soup. The jellyfish were white and small, and so thick that they even brushed by my face. I did have some slight stinging on my lips. What a weird feeling. A few months after our trip to Palau, this lake was closed due to the environmental impact from tourists. I'm so happy that we had the pleasure of this unusual experience.

Bill and I decided to do a night dive in Palau. The one we did in Guam was in shallow water with a small group of friends.

This would be the "real thing". We purchased large hand lights for this special dive.

When we arrived, our favorite boat captain was in charge. Jacques was named for Jacques Cousteau. Despite his youth, he was responsible and experienced. There were six divers and one dive master. Since we did not have advanced dive computer watches, so the dive master asked us to accompany him. We would follow the shallow reef along the ridge line, turn to the left, follow the wall and back to the boat.  It was frightening getting into the water in total blackness. When we turned on our dive lights, a thin stream of light preceded us, breaking through the inky water. It was too late for me to bail.

The dive master had large sized fins and with a couple of kicks, he was out of sight. We were left on our own. We slowly made our way to our left to find the ridge along the reef wall. We followed the ocean floor near the wall. I just knew there were hundreds of sharks out there in the blackness watching us. My ears began popping. Why were my ears plugged? Was Glen still behind me? Lost in my fears, I felt a pull on my fin. I thought it was a shark and was prepared to be eaten. It was Bill.

He pointed to his gauge. I looked at mine. We were at 100 feet and still descending. He pointed at his air gauge. He had 500 psi and I had 700 psi. Normally, at 500psi, the diver would be starting the ascent process. We were running out of air and lost in total darkness in shark infested waters.

Having an innate sense of direction, Bill gestured to follow him. I trusted his instincts. Since we had been in a current, when we changed direction, the current was at our backs. We found ourselves being projected to the surface. At our depth, it was necessary to have safety stops on the way to the surface. Failure to do so, could result in decompression sickness. From 100 feet, we were propelled to the surface without a stop, popping up like corks.

We had no idea how far we had traveled out to sea and

how far we were from our boat. We both began shining our lights in all directions. We were rewarded by blinking lights in the distance and a horn from the boat. While we waited, I wondered where the nearest dive chamber was. I was convinced that little gas bubbles were floating around our bodies looking for a place to land, like our brain. We could have decompression illness.

Jacques helped us up the ladder. He was not smiling. All the divers had returned to the boat. The dive master never approached us or apologized. As they were all waiting for us to surface in the darkness, I'm sure they thought we were lost. Jacques offered us as much water as we could drink and covered us with dry towels. On arrival to the marina, we were the first ones off. We quickly left for our motel.

It was a miracle that we were not injured. We drank quarts of water and stayed warm. We both had splitting headaches. Jacques knocked on our door early in the morning. He was concerned and offered any help we needed.

We spent our last day on a kayak trip in the harbor. Later, we enjoyed shopping in town, buying souvenirs. After a goodbye dinner with Troy and Donna, we packed for our short boat trip to Yap in the morning.

Yap is a thirty-seven square mile island near Palau. It was like going back in time, like Darwin just visited. Eight of us would be staying for two days. We arrived at the dive shop on the edge of the village. Outside the shop on a large wooden board, manta rays were painted, with their individual spots and names. We were here to visit with them underwater.

The dusty paths to our hotel were unkempt. It seemed like everyone was sleeping. Our hotel was the only modern building. The houses had thatched roofs without walls. After dropping off our equipment in our rooms, we all met in the hotel dining room. Along the narrow lawn beside the restaurant were ten-foot circular stones with open centers, like stone cheerios. Our waitress was happy to have customers and sat with us, giving us history about her island.

When the Germans occupied the island, they established a seven-layer caste system still in place today. The society is matriarchal. This system is common in most of the islands. Here in Yap, you can marry up but if you marry down, you stay at that level. The island is divided into individual sectors.

Women did not wear tops until the Peace Corps volunteers visited and T-shirts were encouraged. It is still not permissible to show your legs above the knee. We were cautioned not to wear bathing suits or short shorts in town. This would offend the village elders. An elder will switch your legs if you show disrespect and wear something too short. To visit each small village, the elder must give consent. One of the girls in our group wore a bathing suit in town with exposed thighs. To her surprise, she got her legs switched.

Single men use canes with intricate carvings to indicate their availability and live in Men's houses. Single women live in Women's houses. There are also houses where everyone can gather and hold celebrations. They are all open walled with thatched roofs. On a tour, I noticed the intricate weavings where the roof was joined to the house. I asked about them. There was only one elder who knew how to do the weavings. What a shame to see such a craft disappear.

The locals have a slow day-to-day life. This beautiful island appears depressed and without hope. I purchased a story board in a local shop. These carvings were done on a local hardwood by prisoners. Mine was a deep carving of a woman who owned a breadfruit tree. The written story came with the board. It's one of my treasures.

Stone money was used here for barter in the past. All the houses have various sizes of money in their front yards. The larger the stone, the more valuable. The stone was carved from heated limestone and precariously transported by canoe from distant islands to Yap.

Diving with these mantas draws divers from all over the world. Today was the day we would meet them in person. It was early morning, the sun just warming the air. All the divers were loaded and ready in the dive boat. The dive master explained that every morning, the mantas come into their "cleaning station". They swoop down to clear barnacles from their bodies along the rough surface of the coral.

We were all patiently waiting underwater, our air bubbles noisily rising to the surface. My Zen diving class in Guam was coming in handy. I was sitting on the white sandy ocean floor, at thirty feet, total silence, scattered reflections from the surface of the water shooting rays down to me. With a breath in, my butt barely rose from the sand, breathing out, back down. Perfect balance.

Angels flew in over our heads. Soundless, graceful, smooth, I could see their individual markings and knew how they were named. Dark grey backs and white bellies. Our bubbles rose, bouncing off their bellies. It must have tickled them because they dove low, over our heads. It was like a silent movie. I was a participant in a secret ceremony. It was worth traveling halfway across the planet just to be here.

Bill and I enjoyed their small village shopping area, buying items to remember this unusual island. I found a carved turtle to add to my collection of memories. I purchased a grass skirt, in red, green, and yellow to give my granddaughter.

Soon we were back on a boat to Palau. We would fly to Rota this afternoon. This island is only forty miles from Guam. In WWII, over one thousand Japanese soldiers occupied caves along the shore. They reported movement of U.S. aircraft. I read that the reefs held many downed airplanes and ships.

We found the dive shop and were told that most of the dive spots were off limits. Unexploded ordinance was being removed and the shallow dive areas were affected. Only deep dives were available. Since we were beginner divers, we decided to explore the island.

In a rental car, we found waterfalls, and breathtaking scenery. As we drove, we occasionally saw rusted remains of aircraft in trees tucked away in the forest. A terrible reminder of the loss on both sides.

On a deserted road, we saw a sign for hikes. The owner was repairing a truck in his yard and seemed happy for the company and business. We began our hike uphill, rocky at first then it opened to a slippery uphill grass pasture. We soon came upon the caves hidden in the foliage of the mountain. As we approached, we found the caves were deceivingly large inside. Living in these caves must have been terrible for the Japanese soldiers. Debris of rotted wood and scattered pottery were all that remained from over fifty years ago.

As we were leaving, I spied something green tucked behind some stones. I found a large intact green bottle with Japanese writing on the glass. Another treasure. As we slid down the grass slope on our butts, I hung on to the bottle, determined to get it home in one piece since it had survived the last fifty years.

We left Rota, disappointed that we could not dive, but rewarded by uncovering some of its history

After all our incredible adventures, going home was anticlimactic. In a few months, my contract in Guam would expire. We had added to our library of pictures and mementos these past few years of traveling. We had to decide where to go next. Hawaii maybe?

# CHAPTER 8 ALOHA BIG ISLAND

1997

Bill and I have just arrived on the big island of Hawaii, but it already feels like home. In a matter of days, we found a house to rent. We made an appointment with the owner. Driving up to the address, we found a brown house partially hidden by flowering hedges, and a low stone wall along the road.

The owner, Jeff, came out to meet us. He explained that he is starting a business in Oahu and staying there with his parents. He asked to leave his dog and cat with us. We explained that we had two dogs, and his pets would be no problem.  Jeff then gave us a tour of acres of beautiful gardens. He is a horticulturist and had planted mango, starfruit, breadfruit, water apples, oranges, banana, kumquat trees behind his home.

The house is built Japanese style, in a U-shape. One side is an in-law apartment. The other section is two bedrooms, living room, kitchen, garage with workshop and a jacuzzi on the back deck. In the center of the U is a Japanese garden, perfect in design with small trees and flowering plants. We found a pineapple plant with one just about ready to eat.

After our tour, a mutual agreement on rent was agreed upon. We could move in a couple of days. Three days later, Bill and I moved in with our luggage, planning on picking up our containers from the post office the following day.

The first night at our new home, we tried out our jacuzzi

on the back deck. Lying there in the warm bubbling water, with the multitude of stars overhead, we had truly arrived in paradise. Later we found out that nights in our new home would be drafty. The single wood exterior slats allow cold air through the cracks. Being at 750 feet above sea level is cool. Thank goodness we didn't rent a house higher up on the hill.

My new job in the emergency department was on the night shift. Not being a night person, I'm tired all night and can't sleep well during the day. The hospital was modern and seemed well staffed. The first doctor I met was exceptional and well trained. The night shift was quiet and staffed by two nurses who had been there a long time. They worked together, often taking over my patients and excluding me. Being part of a nursing team for many years, I had experienced this before. I just let them do their thing.

One evening, I took out a journal to read as we had no patients. It was one of my PA journals. I saw them glance at the title, and they began whispering. One of them said to me, "Are you a physician assistant?"

"Yes, I am." And I left it at that. Now I was totally ignored. Performing my duties as safely as possible, I hoped to find a new position soon. Fortunately, it took only three months, and I would be starting a staff position as a physician assistant at a rural clinic in Hilo.

The rural health practice had three clinics and I would rotate on a schedule. The main clinic was in Hilo, a second in Pahoa, and the third in Kau. Pahoa was a fringe town where all the hippies from the sixties went. Kau is a tiny outpost in a far area of the island, the southernmost part of the United States.

My first day I arrived at the Hilo Clinic at seven forty-five for my morning shift. I introduced myself to the charge nurse, Carla. I liked her immediately. There was no doctor that morning, so Carla and I worked together, getting prescriptions called in, and helping me with the new paperwork. At noon, one of the regular doctors arrived and found me in the hallway wearing a white coat and seeing patients.

"Who are you?" rudely asked a short blond woman, wearing a brightly flowered muumuu and flip flops. I had the feeling that this job would be fulfilling as well as interesting.

The next morning, I would meet the medical director. He impressed me as a genuine person with positive goals for the providers and the patients. He was the first person I had ever met from the Marshall Islands.

The town of Hilo reminds me of a town in the mainland in the 1950s. There is one short street with several local shops and restaurants along the edge of a black sand beach. At the corner is the open-air market, busy one day a week with local farmers and crafters. Traffic is light. The second street from the ocean looks a lot like the first, but there are no chain restaurants in sight. A busy Salvation Army on the second street assists many homeless, most of them veterans who live in town or in the woods nearby. As in many larger cities, there is a homeless and drug problem here also.

Our street had four houses, the other three owned by Filipino families who invited us frequently to gatherings of music, singing and lots of food. The house next to us was owned by ginger farmers. The entire side of our house was illuminated as the entire family, adults, and children, cleaned and packed ginger all night for shipping the next day. We marveled at their work ethic and family unity.

We traveled to Oahu after the dogs had been there two weeks. They were jumping in their cages when they saw us. I cried when I saw how skinny they were. We had spoiled them with rice and fish in Guam. We gave them treats and held them. We heard them crying all the way to the parking lot. Two more weeks left in quarantine.

When we arrived two weeks later, we were so happy that

they would be with us. They would have a short plane trip in their cages to the big island. Yelping when they saw us, we put on their collars and leash and took them to the car. At the airport when we put together the cages they were upset. Giving them their favorite chewy treat, they were in their cages and off into the baggage area as we boarded the plane. When we arrived at the house, they were running around the yard and our smiling dogs again. I couldn't wait to fatten them up.

We wanted to include the dogs in our exploration of the island. At first, we traveled to Kona, over the mountain to the tourist side of the island. We found a big warehouse food store where we stocked up on staples. Right next door to the warehouse was Sam Choy's Restaurant. He is a famous Hawaiian chef, and it was our pleasure to eat there many times. The pork dishes were amazing. The dogs waited patiently for us. They always got a treat of hot dogs and buns from the warehouse.

The big island is a paradise with black, green, and white sand beaches. There were uninhabited beaches accessed by paths known by few. Breathtaking waterfalls could be seen along the traveled roads and found in forests. Rainforests hid orchids and birds along lush trails. Coffee bushes lined high mountainsides. We found small towns all over the island, each with its own personality.

The girls weren't happy to get back in cages for the plane trip over to the big island but when they were released in our yard, they ran around for hours. After a couple of days, we had our happy girls back, tongues hanging out and dog smiles.

Bill had found several vehicles on the island, many abandoned in yards. Our garage was turned into a repair center and soon we had more cars than we could ever use. We kept the ones we liked and sold the others.

Our time off was for exploring. One of our favorite towns was Hawi. It was at the northernmost tip of the island. As we entered the town the first time, we found a treasure trove of artisans and a great ice cream store. Paintings, ceramics glassware and unusual handmade items made perfect gifts for our families and souvenirs for us. It took most of the day to drive completely around the island.

The big island of Hawaii is best known for its active volcano. Its two-mile open crater is said to be the firepit and home of Pele, the volcano goddess. A mile wide vent from the bottom of the volcano releases tons of lava daily into the ocean, creating miles of new real estate. The new lava becomes solid and takes hundreds of years to look like normal land.

Bill and I took the dogs to the Volcano Park and walked on the lava fields. There are many visitors walking out on the lava fields, but some have gone out too far and fell through the cracks into the hot lava. Unknown to us, the lava has a fiberglass like substance that hurts the paws of animals. Thankfully, our puppy's paws were not injured. We stayed at sunset and marveled at the red sky over the ocean as the lava poured in sending steam rising from the ocean surface.

In several parts of the island, there are lava spills that permanently covered roads. A recent spill covered homes in the Pahoa and Kau areas.

One of our favorite hikes at Volcano Park is a thirteen-mile hike at an inactive caldera. A short walk through the woods leads to a steep trail downward into the caldera. It's like being on the surface of Mars. Flat lava with steam escaping from vents are at the inside of the caldera. Large heaps of lava and stones are strewn about. The entire time I was walking across the bottom of the caldera, I hoped that Pele was quiet that day. On the far side was another steep trail up into the forest and the trail back around the circumference to our car. It felt like longer than thirteen miles.

When my daughter and her family came for a visit, we hiked the caldera again. Their eyes got wider as they saw where we were going. My seven-year-old granddaughter, Ashley, was the brave one. She loved every minute of the hike. She couldn't wait to tell all her friends back in Maryland that she walked through a volcano on her vacation.

A short while after my family left, Bill had a friend pull into the driveway to talk about a repair on his truck. I heard him call to me. "Hey Jeanne. Come out and see what's in the truck!"

"If it's a puppy, I'm not coming out."

"No, it's not a puppy."

In the bed of the pick-up was a pile of orange mewing kittens. I gave Bill an evil eye. After picking up a tiny kitten, the man said, "That one's yours."

And he was mine, for sure. Blue eyes was named Frankie after Frank Sinatra. After feeding him by bottle, he gradually made his way out into the garage with the three dogs, fast enough to crawl for safety under piles of wood.  One day I saw Sassy holding the kitten by its head, hanging from her mouth. I thought the cat was dead, but Sassy gently put him down in the grass on the lawn. Just taking him for a ride, I guess.

The work at the clinic was busy with routine health care and minor emergencies. There is a large population of diabetes in Hawaii. All the clinicians were urged to adopt a medical issue and become proficient in the care. I chose diabetes and with the help of Melanie, my doctor friend who just graduated from the Cleveland Clinic, I began treating the diabetic patients in our practice.

There was not enough time in a routine visit to educate diabetic patients. Several concerned providers from our area came together and founded a diabetes education center. We volunteered our time for classes in a storefront donated to us, and with the help of a retired nurse, received information from the American Diabetes Association. When I left Hawaii five years later, the center was still active.

On every other Saturday, I covered the clinic in Pahoa from eight till noon. It was the only medical service available on our side of the island except for the emergency room. The line of patients was around the building at opening time. I stopped registration at forty patients. There were always emergencies that needed immediate attention like a baby with a fever of 104. The attached pharmacy filled our prescriptions. I made sticky note notations on charts to complete the chart later after closing. I was usually there for another three hours, completing the charting. It wasn't unusual to have a newborn baby brought in from the homeless in the area. Our Hawaiian registration girls always gave the mother a beautiful Hawaiian name for the baby.

Kau was another favorite clinic. The isolation of this area was depressing and breathtakingly beautiful. It was raw country with cliffs hanging high above the ocean. The people there were so thankful for the medical care. Every day I felt like I had made a difference.

We rarely had visitors since Hawaii is such a distance away from the mainland. When my daughter visited, we flew over to Oahu to visit the Pearl Harbor Memorial. What an experience to see what you had only seen on films. The Arizona wreckage is a memorial site surrounded by walkways around the ship. Oil is still bubbling up to the surface of the water. This memorial leaves an imprint on your heart.

My mother and her friend, Elsie visited, and we returned to Pearl Harbor. They both had husbands involved in wars and were touched to be there. We spent a few days whale watching and walking on Waikiki Beach. When they returned home, they talked about their trip for years.

Our landlord called to ask if it would be a problem if he moved back to his house. There was no deadline to find another place. During our many trips on back roads, we had seen an abandoned plantation house overlooking the ocean. Asking a neighbor near the property, we learned the name of the owner.

He was only too happy to have someone rent and clean the place up.

We moved into our plantation house in the country. On one side was a papaya plantation, across the street was a field with horses. The inside structure was sound, but it needed a thorough cleaning. Fifty gallons of paint later and a good scrubbing it was beautiful. The living room was over twenty feet long. Shining hardwood floors. The kitchen wore new yellow paint and shelving Bill built.

Frankie loved it there. He ran the papaya fields at night and in the morning. left me the heads and feet of the large rats he ate. He was no longer a kitten but a very large cat. The dogs also loved to run through the plantation and in the nearby fields. The owner of the horses in the pasture across the street wasn't too fond of the dogs, however.

The yard was overgrown and the grass up to our knees. We bought a riding lawnmower. I insisted that riding it was my job. When we pulled away branches from the front of the house, we found wild orchids in the trees. We cleaned out the giant underside garage of years of trash.

From our deck, we could see the ocean. The landlord told us that whales could be seen while migrating. We also had a yard with two mango trees, an avocado tree, and several coconut trees. The girls loved to eat the mangos that fell in the grass.

The relationship with Bill had become more strained due to financial disagreements. We could not agree so he left to stay with friends. I remained at the plantation house and continued in the job that I loved. I also liked riding the lawnmower.

My mother was living alone in New Hampshire and withdrawing from family. My grandson in Maryland was ten months old and I had seen him only once. I left the states in 1994 and had been home only for short visits. I needed to return to the real world. Wear regular shoes and long pants, UGH.

Leaving my job at the clinic was heartbreaking. My last two weeks at work, my patients brought gifts and said their goodbyes.

I flew to Florida to rent a house, buy a car, and find a job. Leaving the girls with friends, I was on a flight taking me into the 9-11 nightmare. A couple of weeks later, I returned to Hawaii. The girls, an eighteen -pound Frankie, and I left for Florida and the next chapters of our lives.

# CHAPTER 9
# KONA IRONMAN TRIATHLON

1998 - 2000

No, I didn't do the Ironman Triathlon. I only wish I were in shape to even think about it. However, the next best thing was being able to work with the medical team.

Each year, Kona on the big island of Hawaii holds the Ironman race. In 1997, I traveled with friends to watch my first triathlon and enjoy the atmosphere.

I watched them start for the 2.4- mile open ocean swim in calm water. The course was marked by boats on each side, watching for swimmers in trouble. Divers underwater also watched for injured and sinking divers. They were probably also watching for sharks.

The participants lined up, and at the signal ran into the water with lots of splashing of arms and bare feet. No fins. The group turned at a buoy, less than a dozen in the lead. Soon the leaders ran through either the male or female tent, through a shower, discarding the bathing suit and grabbing shorts, sneakers, and helmets from their aide. They then ran to the line of bikes, assisted with their equipment and getting on bikes. Each participant in the race had an assigned person for safety and speed of transition between events. Their long perilous ride began.

In a flurry of bodies and bicycles, they began their 112-mile ride along the Hawaiian lava desert. This area looks like Mars. Black lava fields as far as you can see to the ocean on the left and hillsides on the right. And to make it more difficult, it is a gradual upward incline. The high speeds come on the way back. When winds are coming off the ocean, they can blow the lighter athletes from their bikes.

Waiting for their assigned athlete, the aide grabbed the bike and assisted with the running gear. Sneakers on, the marathon started --- twenty-six point two miles of pounding the pavement.

As we enjoyed the day, shopping, having lunch, and ice cream, those amazing athletes were out there finishing the race.

We had a great view at the finish line. The crowd went crazy, the music was pumping as the finishers came into view. I swear that the guy who came in first looked like he had just run around the block. It makes you just shake your head in disbelief that a person had trained their body to endure this race.

I applied for a position in the medical tent and got accepted for the 1988 Ironman. Being part of their team was exciting. We were given instructions and waited for our first patients as the race began. The green tent was MASH style with bathrooms and folding stretchers.

As the bikers began their long trip, a few mishaps of bikers crashing into each other occurred. We treated a few scrapes and a couple of broken arms. The scrapes resumed if their bikes worked.

Two women were lifted off their bikes by the wind and thrown into the gulley along the road. The ambulance transported them to us where they were assessed for significant injury that may need the local emergency room. One girl was sobbing in some language I didn't understand. She had a lot of scrapes and bruises, but also a sprained ankle so no marathon for her. The other girl was severely injured. Her neck brace was left on, and she was immediately sent to the ER.

Injuries poured in. There were falls but most problems were due to dehydration. Once the body gets past the dehydration, and has used up all the sugar reserve, it burns fat and then muscle. The body protects itself by redirecting the blood to the inner vital organs. Now the muscles start to fail. Runners who came in for medical attention were severely dehydrated.

IV fluids were started, they were assisted to bathrooms, and sneakers taken off to assess foot damage. There were blisters and ragged nails. The one thing in common was the disappointment that their Ironman race was over for this year.

In 1999, I was accepted as a volunteer along the bike road. Out in the wilderness along the lava desert, there was a station set up for water and bananas for the bikers. My instructions were to stand alongside the road, and when a biker came by, hand them water or banana. There were several of us spaced far apart.

I don't know the actual speed they were traveling, but it was scary fast. Those bikes were hurling at me with an arm out. Throwing a bottle of water into a hand flying at the speed of sound was not easy. I did improve but felt bad for the racers who didn't get water or a banana. It was hot standing on the highway, but I was glad to be part of the team and helping the racers.

In 2000, I volunteered with the ambulance crew. Our job was to pick up runners who were down along the road. They had pushed past their limit. These were mainly the marathon runners. It had been a long arduous day, and for some, mental strength was not enough, and the body shut down. Many were crying in pain and frustration that they were so near the end and couldn't finish.

Athletes who train for these events devote so much time

to being in this elite group. I was amazed at the number of finishers over fifty. If you ever get a chance to watch the Ironman Triathlon, you will be blown away at how fine-tuned these athletes are.  I no longer live in Hawaii, but I watch the Ironman on TV, savoring the memories.

# CHAPTER 10
# FUN RUNS

1999 – 2001

Before moving to Hawaii, I never contemplated running or walking a race. While employed at the Bay Clinic in Hilo, I met Melanie, a physician assigned to our clinic. She was of Hawaiian heritage and was working for four years in the islands to repay medical school. Tina was also new to Hilo, a physician assistant in an orthopedic practice. I met her when I performed her employment physical. It wasn't long before the three of us got together and discovered we all had an interest in racing. Melanie, a native of Oahu, a sister island to the big island of Hawaii, offered to find some racing events there.

Because I wasn't in the best of shape to compete, I began to train. I walked every morning at five at the local high school track. A stopwatch helped me increase my time. My goal was a thirteen-minute mile.

Melanie found us a race coming up in two weeks. It was a 10K woman's race, sponsored by the Straub Hospital in Honolulu. I couldn't wait. I bought a new outfit and started packing immediately. At least I would look good if I came in last. We flew to Honolulu on Friday night and took a shuttle to our hotel.

I told Melanie, "Tina and I are so lucky that you know your way around Honolulu."

"I grew up here and it's really a small island. Even the hotel manager knows my family, so we got a deal on our room."

Tina had never been to Hawaii. At forty-five, she looks and acts twenty. "Where are we eating tonight? Let's have spaghetti so we can carb load before the race tomorrow."

Our hotel room had two king size beds. Overnight bags were thrown carelessly about the room freeing us to enjoy Melanie's tour.

At a brisk pace, Melanie looked over her shoulder at us and said, "First we'll go over to the park at Waikiki Beach and maybe sit in the sun for a bit. There's a good Italian restaurant in walking distance."

Honolulu looks like any other city with traffic and high rises, but when you look closely, the velvet green spiky mountains rise in the distance are spectacular. The temperature is in the seventies, and a warm breeze from the ocean carries a flowery scent. Melanie showed us a tree with pink edged white flowers called frangipani, so fragrant that it's a favorite for making leis.

We walked under the waving palm trees along the beach, sitting on the sand to take in the vista and then strolling through the park to the restaurant. I felt like I was in paradise.

We all gorged ourselves on spaghetti and meatballs and passed on dessert. Melanie told us there's an ice cream store on the way back to our hotel. Twist my arm. We all got double scoops of toasted coconut.

We called it an early night, agreeing that we needed to be rested. The cab would take us to the starting area at six. We agreed to allow each person plenty of bathroom time in the morning before the race, arrive early because the line to the girl's bathroom was usually miles long, warm up together, and forget staying together in the race.

Tina was the last one to join us at the starting area. She got stuck in the long line. Pinning our numbers on and retying our laces, we were excited and ready. When we heard the starting shot, Melanie and Tina were off running. I decided to save my energy for the last part of the race. I began with a slow jog until I tired, then got into my walking pace.

From the starting area at a park, it was uphill on Diamond Head Road. Walking uphill caused me to huff and puff, and I found myself further behind in the pack of hundreds.

Alternating running and walking, I enjoyed the view of surfers below, easily traversing waves. Thank goodness for the volunteers who man the water stations along the race route. Hyperventilation on that hill made me thirsty. The runners discarded the cups on the side of the road. I felt like I was littering.

The race was 6.2 miles. Is doesn't sound like much but at mile five I was so tired that my legs were shaky. Coming downhill with weak legs is scary. If I trip, I'll fall on my face. At last, I saw the finish line, heard the music and people cheering. Not wanting to look like a slow poke, I took a deep breath and walked faster. Forget running.

Melanie and Tina were cheering me on from the sidelines. Their enthusiasm gave me a boost and I jogged over the finish. I paced a 13.17- minute mile. I was happy with that time.

As we walked over the area where the medals would be awarded, Melanie grabbed my arm. "I think I'm going to pass out." We had her lie down on the grass and elevate her legs on a tree. She was pale but smiling. "Thanks, I always faint after racing. I get too dehydrated, I guess."

When the medical staff saw her, they came over to help. We told them that we would hydrate her. We thanked them and after they left, we smiled at each other. Tina said, "I think we've got this medical thing covered."

After changing at our hotel, Melanie took us to a local

shop that made Hawaiian shirts, dresses, and shorts. They were so authentic. We could see people working on sewing machines in the back room. At our clinic, on Fridays, we wore our Aloha shirts with bright Hawaiian colors, and patterns. Next Friday, I would have my own tropical Hawaiian shirt to wear.

Our lunch included a pitcher of Margaritas while sitting on the outdoor deck of the restaurant. All in all, it was a good start to our running careers. After a nap, we dressed for a walk along the beach to find an outdoor restaurant with an ocean view.

Sunday morning, we flew back to Hilo, the race cementing our friendship. Melanie was the designated race finder. We couldn't wait to do this again.

Between races, we had the Volcano Park outside Hilo. It had running trails through forests, around inactive volcanos, and cool air at 4000 feet above sea level. We could train in our back yard, where visitors came to visit from all over the world.

The Volcano Art Center sponsored their 17th Kilauea Volcano Wilderness Run, an exciting annual event on the big island. There were four runs, The Wilderness Marathon is the "world's toughest measured marathon", the Rim Run of ten miles circles the caldera of Kilauea, the Kilauea Caldera Run is five miles along the caldera floor and the Kilauea Caldera 5K Walk for all ages.

On July 1999, Tina, Jean, and I ran completed the 10K. Jean was the wife of the local minister who met Tina at a service. She was excited to join our group. Melanie was disappointed that she had to work. I placed toward the end of the pack with a 14.24-minute mile. The exhilarating part was running through the wooded paths, measuring my breathing, and enjoying music from the local songbirds.

The Dolphin Dash was next. In August, Tina, Jean, and I traveled to Kona to the Hilton Waikoloa Village, a tropical paradise. This incredible hotel was built right on top of lava fields. Long white sandy beaches were joined by smooth aquamarine water. Small, thatched huts lined the beach for a shady nap.

We entered the 5K run/walk. I placed with a 12.28-minute mile at the end of the pack.! Getting better. We thoroughly enjoyed hanging out at the hotel after the race, enjoying all the amenities and came home with trophies and sunburns. Tina got a third place and Jean and I got second in our respective age groups.

Back to Honolulu in August 1999. It was the annual Race for the Cure. This is a big event every year in Honolulu and draws thousands of racers. This race, Tina, Melanie, Jean, and I attended. We flew over Saturday and stayed at our favorite hotel just off Waikiki Beach.

This was an incredibly special race. Cancer participants wore pink, many with pink bandanas or hats covering hair loss. The ceremonies afterwards were heartbreaking but displayed strength and solidarity. We walked as a group just to share the camaraderie of the event.

Four of us decided to train for the Honolulu Marathon that would take place in December of 1999. I found a four-month training program for "How to Walk a Marathon". Melanie declined the marathon but my neighbor, Diane joined our group. The four of us planned to stay together the entire 26.2 miles! We began training in August, six days a week. We met at the track at 5 am. Following the strict guidelines of sprints, hills, and distance, we walked at the volcano when we needed to increase our distances. Toward race time, we were up to 15 miles. It was exhausting and invigorating.

November gave us the opportunity to test our training with a half marathon in Honolulu. Diane, Jean, Tina, and I flew to Oahu on Saturday night. At the crack of dawn on Sunday, we were at the starting line in Kapiolani Park at the base of

Diamond Head Road (uphill again!). I placed at the end of the pack with a 14.07minute mile. At this point in my racing career, I was having serious doubts about a marathon. Not being one to give up or just being stubborn, I was not going to let all my training go to waste. I was on for the marathon.

December came quickly. We were pushing our training. On my 57th birthday on December 11th, the four of us, Diane, Tina, Jean, and I, flew to Honolulu. Jean's husband came with her, and they stayed at the same hotel.  We all carb loaded at an Italian restaurant and went to bed early. Bus service to Kapiolani Park was from 2 to 4 a.m. I was so excited I had trouble falling asleep.

We put out clothing we needed the night before. Our fanny packs were packed with high energy drinks and bars. Hats, band aids, extra socks, and water were ready to go We woke in the morning to a drizzling rain. Borrowing large garbage bags from the hotel, we cut large holes and used them to keep dry until race time.  Any clothing left at the starting line was donated to charity.

The bus from the park would take us to the starting point, downtown Honolulu on the Ala Moana Boulevard. Thousands of runners were standing in the rain. My number was 7100 so you can imagine the starting area with bodies jumping up and down to keep muscles warm. Rain meant wet sneakers and blisters. My feet were already soaked. We looked everywhere for Jean but had to start the race without her.

The serious runners begin in the front. As the race began, it was a long time before we even started to move. The three of us began running slowly. Down paved streets through city blocks with high rises, guards in front of buildings to prevent runners from using bushes, we followed a weaving mass. I had to pee. So did Tina. I spied an alley with dumpsters, no guards. The three of us ran down the alley and crouched behind a dumpster. Other runners must have sensed where we were going and followed us.

As we returned to the street, we looked over our shoulder and saw a stampede headed toward the dumpsters.

Our trio was keeping up with the crowd. We were going at a slow jog. I could feel something between my fourth and fifth toes, like my sock was bunched up. At about mile four, I stopped and took off my sneaker, only to find a large blister. I was told before the race: Never take off your sneakers. You'll never be able to put them back on and continue. I quickly put the sneaker back on and tried to ignore any discomfort.

In about five miles, we were approaching Diamond Head hill. Suddenly we heard someone yelling, "Go to your right. Go to your right." Runners were coming down the hill, sprinting for the finish line. We just looked at each other in amazement. I whined, "They're at the finish and we haven't even gone five miles." Tina and Diane just shrugged, rolled their eyes, and kept on moving.

The miles creeped by. There were water stations, pit stops, more water stations, and sugar snacks for energy. Participants who had stopped to rest lined the roads. They had their shoes off. I wondered who would be giving them a ride back to the start area.

The worst part for me was after mile twenty. I think that this is what's called "hitting the wall". The body is now out of sugar and is burning fat for energy. Fatigue sets in. We began counting out loud when we passed a mile marker. Each marker seemed extremely far away. Runners who had given up lined both sides of the road. Only a few runners could be seen in front and behind us. We were at seven hours and the cut off was eight hours. Would we make it? What happened to all the water stops?

Diamond Head hill was a long steep decline, and on every step, a blowtorch sensation hit my toes. I began talking to myself. I could do this. I was almost there. Just keep going. Put one foot in front of the other.

There were a few stragglers at the finish line cheering us along. Together, we crossed the line at 7:41.52. It was painful to walk to the far end of the park for refreshments, T-shirt, and medal. We found Jean at the refreshments. She finished fifteen minutes ahead of us. When we returned to the hotel, I attempted to climb steps, almost falling when my thigh muscles cramped up. During recuperation, I lost seven toenails and took weeks to recover from leg cramps.

I proudly display my medal in a glass case in my office. I suspect it is the only marathon I will ever finish. A friend mentioned a scenic marathon coming up in a month along the shore in Maui. I thought about it for a nanosecond.

It was a privilege to have lived in Hawaii for five years. The culture and people will be permanently etched in my memory.

In 2001, Sassy, Dutchess, Frankie, and I were ready to move to our new home in Florida.

# CHAPTER 11
# MIDWAY ATOLL

2000

Imagine being invited to an exotic location for a week? The U.S. Wildlife service needed volunteers for one week to count albatross on Midway Island. A co-worker at my clinic in Hilo asked if I would like to volunteer over the Christmas holiday. Of course, I said yes.

The Midway Atoll is more than 1100 miles from Honolulu and the next to last island in the Hawaiian chain. Atoll means a ring-shaped island or reef.

Remnants of the military can be seen on the island. There were high piles of sand where planes were hidden during WWII along the flat terrain. Cement pillbox bunkers decayed by age were spread along beaches. In 1997, the U.S. Navy turned the island over to the U.S. Fish and Wildlife Service. Midway was designated a wildlife preserve for its most important resident...the albatross.

Meg and I received information sheets on what to bring and what duties to expect. Flights in and out are weekly. I checked my supply of film and the telescopic lens on my camera.

Aloha Airlines flies to Midway every Saturday. Meg and I took a flight to Honolulu from Hilo and wandered the airport until we found our gate and our "puddle jumper". Finding our seats, we were approached by other volunteers who had been to Midway before. We all became so engrossed in the conversation, that we didn't even notice the wheels leaving the ground.

My first view of Midway from the plane took my breath away. This jewel is isolated in the middle of a green ocean. As we neared, I could see the island was flat with tufts of grass and sandy areas. Large sections were occupied by birds, Black and white birds, chicken-sized, covered the ground as far as I could see. Someone must have cleared the runway because the birds were right along the edge of the tarmac. Our job this week was to count these birds to determine if the population is increasing or decreasing. I felt the bump of the landing and anxiously awaited beginning my week here.

We found a building marked, "Barracks". Our new home for a week. Meg and I quickly unloaded our gear. We had two metal beds, like camp, with bathrooms across the hall shared by other volunteers. We hurried to the building we were told was the mess. Today we would have lunch, meet all the volunteers and staff, and find out about the week ahead.

The aroma of freshly baked bread and cookies led our way to the mess hall. Picking up a tray, cafeteria style, I began slowly moving along the line, stopping frequently, unable to choose from the selections. I hadn't even gotten to the bread and dessert yet. At the very end – several choices of real ice cream with toppings greeted me. I guess I'll punch another hole in my belt.

Our guides were informative and seemed to be excited to be here with us. We would be going out tomorrow at 8 a.m. After lunch, we met in the volunteer center to watch a film on conservation efforts at Midway. Since it was near Christmas, dinner in the mess was followed by a holiday party with all the staff and volunteers.

When Meg and I arrived at the meeting center, we found a beautifully decorated Christmas tree, an open bar, loud Christmas carols and pool tables. Since visitors were rare on the island, we were all welcomed as family. I had no problem finding a pool partner. Although it was not a traditional holiday celebration, Meg and I agreed that we had a wonderful evening, an exciting way to ring in our new year.

The next morning, each group lined up shoulder to shoulder, everyone holding an orange paint gun. We walked along a strip of land in front of us, squirting a dob of paint on each nest while counting. At the end of the row, the number would be written down by the captain of the group, then another line formed. The nests were so thick that we had to step over the bird incubating the eggs.

Albatrosses are also called gooney birds. They come by their name rightly. When they take off and land, they look drunk. They have "aerial grace and earthly clumsiness" as stated in the brochure.

The albatross mates for life. One sits on the nest as the other flies off to collect food. When it returns, sometimes several days later, it feeds the regurgitated food to the mate. We found Bic lighters around the perimeter of the nest. The lighters float in the ocean and collect snails. The gooney bird eats them and when they evacuate around the nest, the lighter is expelled. Unfortunately, large items like lighters can be fatal.

At this time of year, the eggs were still being incubated. Goony babies are the cutest fluff balls. I was disappointed that our group would not be here when the eggs hatched.

I didn't mind being sweaty and tired at the end of the day. I was contributing something important to nature preservation. My sneakers were decorated with orange splotches. Mealtimes were filled with conversation and laughter. No complaining was heard.

Some evenings we attended movies and lectures about the island's inhabitants and their future. We learned that several other species of animals are studied here. They include a variety of birds, monk seals, green sea turtles, spinner dolphins and local fish. Maybe I could come back to study the turtles? That looked like fun.

Meg and I found a small settlement of homes occupied by permanent residents. They are mostly government workers and some wildlife service staff. We agreed that this would be a lonely job. The gift shop had an abundance of literature, clothing, and souvenirs. We went there to rent bikes and decided we would be back to shop.

As we rode our bikes along a well-traveled path, we agreed that if we kept going along the beach in the same direction, we couldn't get too lost. After all, it's an island, right?

We found frigate birds with their red chests puffed out like balloons. Cute small white birds called boobies had either red or blue feet and bills. Multicolored canaries surround us in the low trees. Their singing is like a chorus of different songs. We asked on our return why there were so many and were told that in 1910, a family who lived here released their 12 pet canaries. The have since multiplied to more than 500.

Along the deserted quiet beaches, we saw abandoned guns and pillboxes. As we rode our bikes, we would occasionally find patches of a runway where sand was blown away. It was so peaceful with only the sound of waves and birds singing. It was difficult to imagine war ever touching this place.

We were told by the residents here that there is a French restaurant on the beach. Go figure. It truly was a gourmet French restaurant owned and operated by two castaways living in paradise. I had scallops that melted in my mouth one night and ordered the fresh lobster the next visit. I grew up in New England being spoiled by Maine lobster. This was far superior, even without butter.

The endless fine white sandy beaches are joined by crystal-clear green water. Currents sweep past this tiny island, depositing refuse from the rest of the world on the beach. Fishing nets, buoys, plastic bottles, and even medical waste piled high on the beach made you want to cry. We had to wear sneakers on the beach for safety.

One evening, several of us decided to walk after dinner. It was just before sundown. One of the guys asked, "Hey guys. Have you ever seen a green flash?"

"What's a green flash?" Meg asked.

Parker, who is a volunteer and world traveler, spoke up. "As the sun sets and the instant it breaks the horizon, there will a green flash. This is only seen under certain atmospheric conditions, especially if the sky is clear. This island is so isolated we should see one.

I looked at him and rolled my eyes. "You're kidding us, right? There's no such thing."

Nodding his head and smiling, he said, "You'll see."

We all sat on a large piece of driftwood and concentrated on the horizon. Tonight, the horizon was clear and crisp. Just as the tiny edge of the sun disappeared, there it was. I saw it. An instantaneous green flash.

I jumped up and down. "I saw it. I saw it. Did anybody else see it?"

Everyone was smiling. "Yes, Jeanne, we saw it."

Parker came over, put his arm around my shoulder, and as we walked back toward our dorms, he said, "That trip down the beach was totally worth it to see how happy that green flash made you."

This week was one of the most enjoyable of my life. I'm not planning to wash my sneakers. Those orange spots remind me of my voyage into history.

# CHAPTER 12 WHERE WERE YOU ON 9-11

2001

If you asked this question of anyone who was old enough to recall that day, you would probably get an immediate response. I was uncomfortably close to the events.

A resident of Hilo Hawaii for five years, I decided to move back to the mainland. My destination was Tampa. There, I planned to buy a car, rent a house, and set up nursing jobs. I left Hilo the morning of September tenth bound for Honolulu. My next flight was overnight to Newark, New Jersey. I was due to land in the morning of September eleventh.

My dogs, Sassy, and Dutchess were staying with my friend, Charlotte. Frankie the cat had plenty of rats to catch in the papaya field near our home. My neighbor would leave out cat food at intervals in case he got lazy. I would miss his disgusting gifts of heads and feet of his captures, left at the kitchen door.

While waiting for my first flight, I made notes to remind myself of the many tasks I needed to complete in Florida. I love to people watch in airports. While sipping a caramel Frappuccino, I noticed a black man in a clerical robe nearby. I wondered if he was a priest and if so what kind. His robe was trimmed with red---maybe a bishop? He was sitting with a woman. Maybe he was a Protestant cleric?

Two small children were screaming and running up and down the aisle, assaulting my eardrums. How much do you want to bet they're sitting behind me for a few thousand miles? The boarding announcement interrupted my thoughts.

The aisle seat was already taken. A middle-aged attractive lady smiled as I sat down. I settled into the center seat, getting out my water and the new publication of *SCIENTIFIC AMERICAN*. She said, "Hi, my name is Joanne. Here's your end of the seat belt. It looks like a packed plane today."

"Yes, it's sure crowded. Thanks for the help. What's your destination?"

Joanne replied, "I'm bound for Boston to visit my family for the first time in seven years. I can't wait to see them. How about you?"

"My final destination is Tampa."

The flight attendant announced that everyone needed to get settled and began closing the overhead cabinets. Joanne and I continued our conversation while the flight waited in line to take off. She lived in Maui with her boyfriend and worked in real estate.

On long flights like this, I usually read a magazine or one of several new novels I take on trips. I read until I fall asleep. I'm always hoping I don't snore or drool on my neighbors. Call me insecure.

Reading was interrupted by mealtimes and late evening snacks. The lights dimmed and Joanne and I called an end to our conversation. I usually don't like to talk to other passengers, but she and I developed a friendship.

The children I was worried about were quiet the entire flight. Better yet, they were way in the back of the plane. I became aware of morning when Joanne pushed up her window shade. In the distance, the sky was flushed pale pink behind white, fluffy clouds.

I could smell coffee. The rattling cart came down the aisle.

Flight attendants, looking fresh after a long night, served coffee and warm washcloths. Feeling the warmth on my face feels luxurious. Why don't I do this at home? Soon, breakfast was served. I chose small pancakes with syrup and another coffee. Joanne and I resumed our conversation and soon the flight attendants cleared our trays.

Conversation was humming as everyone woke up. There was a lot of traffic up and down the aisles to the rest rooms. People were rummaging around in the overhead for dental items and new reading material.

There was a loud "ding" from the PA system. "This is your captain speaking. Our plane is being diverted to an alternative airport. We will be updating you with more information as soon as possible."

There was a sudden silence in the plane, followed by cell phone conversations.

I glanced at Joanne. Her eyes were bigger. She was pale and her hands were trembling. "What do you think is happening, Jeanne?"

Before I could answer, the captain was speaking. "This is your captain. We have been informed that our diversion is due to a plane that has just struck the World Trade Center. Our destination is an alternative airport in Middletown, Ohio."

The conversation volume increased as people called their friends and families. Flight attendants did not stop anyone from using cellphones. Probabilities abounded. Strangely, there was no information sharing.

Joanne began to cry. "I don't know where I'll stay in Ohio. I don't have any money for hotels. Where is Ohio, anyway?"

I tried to calm her, despite my own anxiety. "We'll stay together. I can help with the hotel bill. We'll figure out a way to get to our destination. I can always rent a car."

We sat quietly, absorbed in our own thoughts. The stressful mood was interrupted by the captain.

"This is the captain speaking, folks. Just letting you know that we will be landing at the Middletown Airport in less than one hour."

There was no further information. Joanne and I tried to keep busy by packing up our books and sweaters into our carry-on bags. We were silent, with our own thoughts and fears as we waited.

I heard and felt the engines change speed. The plane turned and my ears began popping with the altitude change. Joanne and I shared her window as we watched the plane lower to an altitude where we could see the airport in the distance.

As a physician assistant in Connecticut, I worked at Bradley International Airport medical facility. I knew a little about airports and could see that this was a small airport to land this big plane. As we approached the ground, I could see people lining the runway with cameras. I didn't see rescue vehicles. That would have really scared me.

Our plane landed, brakes screaming. As the plane came to a stop near the terminal, a truck appeared and towed our plane to a distant corner of the airport tarmac, far away from everyone and everything. That made me nervous.

Joanne's anxiety went into high gear. "Oh my God. How long will we have to sit out here? Do you remember the plane in France that sat on the runway for three days and the toilets overflowed?" She was wringing her hands and crying.

"Maybe it's a high jacking but I haven't seen anybody strange in the plane get up and walk to the captain's area. We'll just have to wait until we find out what's happening." In my mind I was also thinking a bomb scare. Nothing I could have conjured up would match the reality of what was really happening.

That hour of waiting was stressful. The truck returned and slowly, pulled us back to the terminal. As the plane stopped, Joanne grabbed my arm. "Look outside, Jeanne. Men with guns are standing around the plane."

Men in uniforms with machine guns had surrounded the plane. As we walked down the stairway, they continued pointing the weapons at us. The long line of passengers entered the terminal where we were greeted by FBI and interviews. We still didn't know what was happening.

Over my shoulder while exiting the plane, I saw a police car with a passenger in the back seat, the black cleric I saw in Honolulu. This was a day you didn't want to look different.

Joanne and I took a seat near the employee lounge where we could hear a television. We heard that a second plane had hit the other tower. I knew then that it was not an accident. I suddenly felt fear and nausea. Neither of us spoke, too caught up in our thoughts.

We were taken as a group to busses lined up at the curb. Each bus had a hotel destination depending upon hotel availability. Airline representatives assured passengers that the first night would be covered by the airline. We arrived at Best Western, tired, and scared. Checking in using my credit card, we arrived at our room.

The air conditioning and silence were welcoming. We threw ourselves on our bed and turned on the television. We were mesmerized. Despite the horrible scenes, we couldn't tear ourselves away from the screen. We cried. We called our families. We worried.

As our country's tragedy unfolded, we felt fortunate that our plane was not involved. The days dragged. There were no rental cars. There were no flights.

On the third day, the desk informed us that a shuttle could take us to the airport in Columbus, Ohio, where we could rent a car. We packed quickly. There were only twenty passengers that could fit in the shuttle, and we got a seat. We arrived at a Motel 6 and checked in. Immediately, I was on the phone.

A compact car rental was arranged for delivery to the hotel the next morning at eight. Joanne called the Greyhound Bus Station. She would be leaving for Boston at eleven in the morning. I planned to drop her off at the bus station.

We were so relieved to have solid plans to resume our trip. Our mutual decision to turn off the television and relax that afternoon was interrupted. A loud knock on the door broke our tranquility.

When I opened the door, a giant Hawaiian man in a red floral shirt, light blue shorts and sandals blocked the door. Politely and with a wide smile, he introduced himself. "My name is Earl."

Joanne just stared at him. I sensed a gentle giant.

"My mother and I were told that a lady rented a car to travel to Florida. Someone told me it was you. I thought we could share expenses since we are both going that way."

"Yes. Where are you going in Florida?"

"Our family is in Fort Lauderdale. I can rent a car if you're not going near there."

I told Earl, "I can let you off in Orlando. You could rent a car there. Why don't we all have dinner tonight in the hotel at six. I can meet your mother and we could make all the arrangements?"

Earl replied, "That sounds nice. My mother would like that. See you at six."

Joanne and I arrived at the restaurant at six to find Mary and Earl already there. Mary had on a bright blue Hawaiian print muumuu. She was as tiny as Earl was large."

We all enjoyed the conversation. Mary was quiet but when she spoke, her voice was strong and engaging. They were very polite. Plans were put in motion to meet at my car at eight in the morning.

When Earl arrived on time, he had three suitcases, a wheelchair and Mary. I had no idea that she needed a wheelchair. Visions of fitting it into my compact car whirled in my head. I also knew that I would not be making a fast trip to Florida. After all the events happening in the country, the least I could do was help stranded travelers.

It was a jigsaw puzzle to pack, but with everyone's laps packed high, we left for the Greyhound station. Joanne and I said our goodbyes and promised to keep I touch. I reshuffled the baggage. We were off.

Normally, I would have driven straight through. It was at least fourteen hours, but I've done that in the past. Mary required frequent stops and we rested at mealtimes. At the first restaurant, soon after we were seated, Earl got up. He began shaking hands with patrons and introducing himself. As our food was delivered, he took my hand and Mary's, saying grace.

I am not a religious person. At all. This made me extremely uncomfortable. As we resumed our trip, a ukulele miraculously appeared in Earl's hands. He began strumming. He and Mary began harmonizing. He smiled at me. "Mary and I are Evangelical and sing at our church in Hawaii."

Mary was a sweet person. I probably could have picked her up easily she was so small. Dressed in floral muumuus, contrasted by her dark Hawaiian skin, she was a postcard for the Hawaiian culture. The wheelchair was for long distances. Her singing voice was clear, and she and Earl did sound heavenly.

And so, for two days, I was serenaded with religious songs along the highway. It was a very, very, long trip.

Earl confided in me that he had never driven on a

highway. He was going to rent a car in Orlando and drive to Fort Lauderdale. Not a long trip but he would have to navigate freeways and highways. During the drive, I attempted to show him how to stay in the center lane, how to exit and enter the roads, and explained signs. I did not have much confidence in his skills.

When we arrived in Orlando, I found a hotel for them and stayed while they registered. The hotel clerk made a call for a rental car for Earl. A bystander took our picture. We exchanged addresses and I was off to Clearwater, the other side of the state. I was so anxious to complete my long list of duties and return home to Hawaii to my life and my pets.

The trip back to Hawaii was uneventful. The airports were very changed. Security was strictly enforced. Lines were long. Driving up to my plantation house, I was filled with gratitude for my life.

I received a letter from Earl one month later. He had a problem with directions. He became lost but found a policeman near Lake Okeechobee, in the opposite direction from his destination. The police called his family. Earl's cousin was a state trooper who came to their rescue.

It's now time to pack and say my goodbyes to the friends I made here on this beautiful island paradise.

# CHAPTER 13 BACK TO THE MAINLAND

2001

My flight to Florida on 9/11 was to find a job, purchase a car and rent a house. I returned to Hawaii to pack up my belongings. The pets would require paperwork before they could travel. Thank goodness they weren't with me on the 9/11 flight.

I often think back to the events surrounding 9/11. I know everyone recalls where they were on tragic moments in history. My plane diversion during this tragedy was inconvenience only. The worse moments for me were seeing people jumping out of windows on TV. That image will never leave my mind. Joanne, the girl sitting next to me on that flight, has kept in touch. Sharing an event like that creates special relationships. We are still sharing letters twenty years later.

After four years in Hilo, Bill and I parted ways. He refused to find a job and contribute to our expenses. His money from car repairs was insufficient and had always been the source of many arguments. A high school reunion in New Hampshire with a side trip to the Cayman Islands for diving had already been paid for and was non-refundable. We took the trip but were barely speaking.

The twelve days were stressful. There were times when he clenched his fists, his face reddening, just staring at me. When we returned to Hawaii, our last conversation before he packed his bags and left was frightening. He told me how he had planned to kill me while traveling through a rural part of New Hampshire.

Leaving behind a huge credit card bill for me to pay, he finally left to stay with friends. I heard that he wore out his welcome with our friends, promising them a business proposition and reneging. I heard that he also left the island on September 10th.

Before I left, I spent a few months living in the plantation house alone and loved it. Using the riding mower fed my desire to become a race car driver. The huge estate was a labor of love but a lot of work for one person.

I wrapped up my job, sold my car and furniture. I mailed my usual cartons ahead to the post office in Dunedin, Florida.

I rented a nice house in Dunedin, lined up a job as a traveling nurse, and purchased a new Subaru that I left at the Tampa Airport. When I returned with the animals, I would pick up my new car.

Frankie was now sixteen pounds and was not likely to appreciate being in a travel bag. After visiting the vet and discussing dosages of tranquilizers, Frankie would be making the trip in a kitty coma, in a travel bag at my feet in the airplane.

On travel day we all needed a tranquilizer. The puppies were placed in their cages at the Hilo Airport for their journey to Dallas. They would be given to me in the terminal for loading to Tampa. The poor dogs were so confused while we were all waiting in the terminal in Dallas. Thank goodness they were loaded first with the luggage.

Frankie was another story. I was afraid that I would kill him with the tranquilizer, so I gave him just a little dose every few hours. At the airport ladies room in Dallas, I gave him another dose. He was limp when I picked him up out of his carrier but breathing well. I was so afraid that he would come to life and run through the terminal. I dosed him again and wondered if I should also take a small dose.

The Tampa airport had wheelchair attendants. Fortunately, I found one to assist me. He waited with the dogs until I returned with my car. At the first opportunity, I found a grassy area for them to relieve themselves and walk around a bit. We were off to our new house in Dunedin. Frankie slept soundly for the entire trip.

The realtor had not left the keys as discussed. He could not be reached. We all slept in our new car that night.

Life became routine again. The dogs had a fenced in back yard. Frankie was free to roam. He was an outdoor cat, used to running in the papaya fields in Hawaii. He could not be expected to live indoors. Being a super smart cat, he found his way home at mealtimes. No big rats to bring home like in the fields back home.

My job in the emergency room was busy as expected. I began my odyssey to obtain my physician assistant license in Florida.  The state required verification of every license I had ever held, both RN and PA. This involved eight US licenses for RN., and USVI, Guam, Hawaii. They also required verification of PA licenses, four US licenses and Guam and Hawaii. I paid each licensing board for the paperwork.

As I contacted the board, I was told verification papers were not all returned. I had the phone numbers and names for licensing boards in every state, calling them often to find out when my paperwork would be sent out. Just as it looked like I was getting close, the inept staff at the board would tell me, "Oops", they needed something else. This went on for eight months. I cried with relief the day my license was approved.

My agency and travel nursing jobs were intermittent. Finances were difficult. Some of the jobs I accepted were so bad that I was concerned about my license. Agency nurses and travel nurses are often hired to supplement staffing problems. At times it seemed that there were too many patients and not enough time to properly care for them.

Friends recommended me to a physician working in a family practice in Wauchula, Florida. Dunedin is on the west coast of Florida and Wauchula is in the center of the state. Farm country. No ocean. Since leaving South Carolina in 1994, I had always been near the ocean. But since this job was available, I gratefully accepted the position.

My rental house was surrounded by fields with cows. I looked for the cute new calves every morning. I hadn't gotten to the desperate point yet that I'd named the cows. My dogs were sniffing at an area of the back deck. When I looked around, I found a gigantic hole leading under the wood. My landlord told me it was probably a snake. Why does it need such a big hole?

When I found a black snake with red stripes that had come up through the drain in my shower, that was it. The snake story is red on black, venom lack, red on yellow, kill a fellow. It may have not been poisonous, but it was time to move. I didn't like the job anyway.

The physician that hired me in Wauchula had friends in Port Canaveral who were opening a satellite clinic associated with the Kennedy Space Center. When I interviewed, I found that one of the doctors was an avid scuba diver. We bonded and I was hired on the spot.

In Port St. John, I found a rental house. Driving my own U Haul, I moved the few pieces of furniture I had acquired. I introduced Frankie, Sassy, and Dutchess to our new home.

I love my new job. The practice is Occupational Medicine. I am performing commercial driver's exams and assisting with FAA and Border Patrol physicals. We also immunize Space Center employees leaving the country. Cruise ship staff obtain physicals and lab work at our clinic. Nicer yet, I make more money.

Within three months, I found a house to buy in Port St. John. It was a red brick house with lots of overgrown trees. It needed lots of TLC. I couldn't wait to start fixing it up. This was the first home I purchased by myself.

My family was still in New Hampshire. My brother called me about my mother who was not doing well in assisted living. She now refused Sunday dinners with his family and there was a question about her taking her medications. I arranged to visit with her and found her depressed. Thankfully, she agreed to move in with me in Florida. I enticed her with being able to sit on the porch in the Florida winter sunshine.

She moved in with me in the fall of 2004. I accepted her decision to decline dialysis for her kidney disease. I hoped that she would enjoy living in Florida. We had frequent lunches out, went to movies and plays, and shopped at Penney's. She always complained that I pushed her wheelchair too fast. She said it with a smile.

I admit that I wondered about living with my mother for the first time since I was seventeen. There were a few standoffs over who would do what household chores, but otherwise we got along well. Not easy with two stubborn women in the same household.

Frankie had a reputation for being a neighborhood pest, leaving footprints on car hoods. During a routine exam, the vet found that he had been shot with BBs. He was also found locked in a neighbor's shed after being missing for two weeks. When I found him one afternoon, lying dead on my bed, I suspected he had been poisoned by aggravated neighbors. I cried for days.

While I was still missing Frankie, two new kittens moved in. Bert was black, Ernie an orange tabby like Frankie. With her knitting and two lap cats, mom was kept busy and happy while I was at work.

I scolded her for not eating lunch. She would tell me she

had an apple. To make sure she had something more substantial, I had a neighbor stop by around lunchtime every day to "visit". While there she would offer to make lunch. Never one to complain, my mother told me one evening, "You know, Sally comes over every noontime and interrupts my TV shows. She also wants to make my lunch." So much for a good idea.

As the kidney disease progressed, constant supervision was needed. Either I quit my job to stay home or used assisted living. I found a single-family home that was converted to provide care to four people. My mom was now in Hospice and this home was highly recommended.

I visited three times daily and stayed at night until she fell asleep. Her condition worsened over the next month. Several family members were able to visit before she was gone. A big loss, my surviving parent. My house was empty. Soon, it was time to move on.

Where to go? I thought I might like to return to Myrtle Beach. I accepted a position at an urgent care clinic there. While preparing to move, I allowed a co-worker to send my resume to a practice in Bloomington, Indiana. Within days, they offered to pay my way there to interview.

Their family practice was one of the largest in the area and busy. The owner made me an offer I couldn't refuse. I accepted the offer, but I had to call the clinic in Myrtle Beach and decline the position. Very embarrassing.

In April 2007, I began working at the family practice in Indiana. It was not a good fit. The medical ethics were questionable to me. I resigned just before a local hospital bought the practice.

Bloomington is a college town. There was so much to do there. Not wanting to leave the area, I accepted a job with Hospice. I had not lived in a winter climate for many years. The wind blowing across Indiana starts in the Rockies and nothing stand in its way across the middle of the country.

Hospice means home visits. Bloomington is rural and I was on the road visiting patients in the country. It wasn't long before I realized I needed warmer clothing. I found a military like parka with fur around the hood at Salvation Army. Medical scrubs are cotton. They are not warm in temperatures in the teens with high winds and blowing snow. Although I found Hospice rewarding and loved interacting and supporting families undergoing terminal illnesses, warmer weather won out. I called that friend in Myrtle Beach. The offer was still open.

Just prior to moving, Sassy became ill. She began having a seizure. I panicked. I can deal with people having a seizure but not my dog. After a couple of calls, I was on my way to an animal emergency hospital fifty miles away in Indianapolis. In blizzard conditions with her seizing in the back seat all the way, by some miracle I found the hospital. They were wonderful. She stayed for three days, diagnosed with a brain tumor.

After medications, she was alive but a shell of the personality she had before. She came home to be with us. She and Dutchess sat on the front lawn watching cars go by, wandered the back fields behind the house and in one week, she was gone. Both Dutchess and I were devastated.

I packed all my furniture and most of my belongings in a POD and had it transported to Myrtle Beach for storage. I called my brother to help me move. The snow was knee deep the day we packed the rest of my stuff in the U Haul. I think I should buy stock in that company. I left Indiana for Myrtle Beach.

My brother, Ralph, is a great guy. Always there to help me. I'm so lucky to have him. With Dutchess, Bert, and Ernie in my car, he drove the U Haul and I followed. We all arrived at a friend's house and unloaded the U-Haul into her garage. Ralph traveled back to New Hampshire the following day. He's used to the snow. Not for me! I'm back in Myrtle Beach. Maybe it gets as low as the thirties in the winter but no blowing snow. Ralph and

I traveled from forty degrees in Bloomington to sixty in Myrtle Beach.

After two weeks, my best friend in real estate found me a perfect house. Dutchess, the cats, and I moved into our new home in April 2008.   No, I'm not done traveling. Found a brochure for a one-week live aboard dive trip to Puerto Rico over Christmas. It's warm there!

# CHAPTER 14 SCUBA DIVING IN BONAIRE

2004

Everything about my job in Florida in a satellite clinic for Kennedy Space Center was a huge change. No ambulances arriving at the back door of an urgent care clinic, no crying children with earaches. This job was occupational medicine, performing hearing tests, commercial driving exams, and a variety of new procedures.

Beth, an employee at the medical facility at Kennedy Space Center was loaned to our clinic on occasion when we were short staffed. She was a ball of sunshine. On the first day we worked together we discovered that we both liked to scuba dive. I was so excited when she invited me to join the Kennedy Space Center scuba club and invited me to attend their next meeting. It was reassuring to have a new friend.

The annual dive destination was Bonaire, a Dutch island in the Caribbean Sea, fifty miles off the coast of Venezuela. When the dates were announced, Beth and I were the first ones to sign up. My last dives were in Hawaii, three years ago. Beth's last dive was a year ago in Bonaire. We were so excited to be going on a trip that we left the meeting and splurged on beer and greasy hamburgers. That was when we decided we needed to lose a few pounds before the trip.

You've heard the saying, opposites attract? Beth and I were certainly opposite. I was a detail person, yes, a little OCD. She was carefree, with a whirlwind around her. Always late, losing things, but one of the most endearing friends I ever had. We found humor in everything.

The first thing on our "to do" list was checking our dive equipment, so I offered to drop it off at our local dive shop. Neither of us wanted to miss dives, or worse, have a medical problem.

Passports in order, equipment checked, and tickets purchased, we were ready to go. On the way to the airport, Beth couldn't find her driver's license. I pulled over while she checked through her large knapsack. Finally, after pulling out a mass of clothing, snacks, and toiletries, she excitedly said, "I found it!" We arrived to find our group in our flight's departure lounge.

Our dive group was an interesting mix of doctors, engineers, and a collection of space center employees. Most of them had been on this trip to Bonaire in the past. Conversation during the trip centered around dive stories. The corals and fish they described reminded me of Palau.

We arrived in the early afternoon, cruising into the airport in clear blue skies. Seeing the island below from the plane, it looked so small and surrounded by shallow reefs and white sandy beaches. The airport name was Flamingo International Airport, the symbol of the island. The airport tower is painted flamingo pink.

Beth and I collected our luggage and left with our group to our bus. I had no idea that Bonaire was dry with cactus spreading across dry desert. Smoky mountains could be seen in the distance. It looked like Arizona.

We passed through a small town with one intersection. Beth pointed out the colorful shops along the main street. "That one is the best for buying souvenirs. There's the grocery store to get fruit for snacks. And there is the ice cream store, where we can walk every night for the best ice cream."

"How far is the hotel from downtown?" I asked.

Beth remarked, "Just a short walk. The walk feels good after a long day of diving. Sometimes a group gets together and does a night dive. I've never joined them. I'm terrified of the dark water and sharks."

"I'm with you. I'll pass on the night dives." I still get anxious thinking about the disastrous night dive in Palau.

Thankfully, we have single rooms. I would not be able to tolerate the clutter from two people for a week. Wet bathing suits and dive gear from one person in one small bathroom can sure accumulate in a week.

Buddy's Dive Shop was well known to divers visiting Bonaire. The shop was huge with a vast array of t-shirts, dive gear and a maintenance shop. Beth told me their dive masters are the best. At dinner, we met some of them over drinks in the bar. Our first dive was in the morning, and we needed to get some rest and start hydrating.

I knocked on Beth's door in the morning and found her still sleeping. Promising to meet me at breakfast, I only hoped that she wouldn't miss breakfast and the dive. Arriving in a rush, Beth managed to make herself a biscuit and ham sandwich before returning to her room to collect her gear.

At the dock, everyone was talking about today's dive. Since we had been in an airplane at several thousand feet, the first dive today would be shallow. The dive master called, "Attention". He told the group that today we would be diving near the dive shop, a shallow dive to colorful corals and fish. In the afternoon, the boat would take us out a few miles from shore for a reef dive at sixty feet.

As Beth and I prepared our equipment, laughing that our dive suits that were snug. Apparently, we didn't lose much weight. All went well as we entered the water and began descending. Then, Beth gave me the sign that she was returning to the surface. She was having a problem with her mask staying on. We aborted the dive. The boat crew radioed to the dock to send a boat out for her. After a quick fix at the dive shop, she was back and ready for our dive. We paddled around at twenty feet near the boat, enjoying just being in the water. Our dive group had left the area.

At lunch, I encouraged Beth to check items she hadn't sent to the repair shop at home. I was concerned her old second-hand equipment would result in an injury during a dive. Even a loose strap on a flipper can cause a dive to be aborted.

Taking it all in stride, she consented. All checked out, she was ready for the afternoon dive. It was amazing. We swam along a sandy coral shelf at twenty feet to the edge of a two hundred foot drop off. Coral gardens of purple, pink and gold six-foot-long tube sponges were glorious. Beth pulled on my hose, pointing to a hawkbill turtle gliding overhead. Schools of colorful tropical fish swan by, ignoring us while on their leisurely swim. The dive was over too soon.

Breaking through the surface after a dive is exhilarating. Leaving one world and entering another. Fresh air. Salty water. Now, getting up on the boat.

There's a lot of equipment to wear as a scuba diver. The jacket is large and can be inflated. Hoses join the jacket to the large tank of compressed air tied to a plastic board on your back. One hose supplies air to your jacket, the BC, that can be inflated and deflated for buoyancy. The other hose supplies air to the diver through a mouthpiece. A snorkel mask is worn over the eyes and nose. Large flippers help propel the diver through the water.

When getting into the boat, the flippers are held in one hand while the other hand grabs an attachment on the boat, like a bar or railing. When you're ready, the person on the boat grabs the tank top and helps lift you onto a step or a platform. Beth and I are both "bottom heavy", which makes our exit from the water not very glamorous.

Our next morning is a special dive. It's called the dive of a thousand steps. Beth jokingly told me to rest up. I would need all my energy for the steps. There really were only sixty-four steps. At least the dive team carried our air tanks up and down the steps.

Struggling back up the stairs after our dive, the hot sun was baking our heads. We had to carry our own jacket, hoses, mask, and fins. By the time we arrived at the dive bus, our faces were bright red and sweaty. The sport of diving does not encourage the use of make-up.

Two dives a day requires a lot of energy. The time below the surface is precious and brief. The work part is getting in and out of the water. Today after our first dive of the day, we took just a few minutes to grab a sandwich and a much-needed nap.

The afternoon dive was a site five miles offshore. The boat ride was relaxing and the breeze welcoming. Our dive was on a shallow coral reef. Beth and I cruised at thirty feet, hands clasped on our bellies, floating in a weightless paradise of fish, corals, and silence. We practiced our buoyancy by rolling on our backs and performing somersaults. Such freedom.

That evening we ambled down to the ice cream stand for a double scoop. Being glamorous and thin were temporarily forgotten. We must be burning calories with all our exercise. We shopped at the grocery store and found some local tiny, sweet bananas. My guess was that Beth fell asleep as soon as I did after returning to our rooms.

I chose to do an early morning dive while Beth went on the regular dive. Up at five, I had coffee in the restaurant and met three other early risers. We opted for a shore dive off the boardwalk in the marina.

The sun was just peeking over the pink horizon. We entered the water and began to cruise along a coral studded reef at thirty feet. With the reef over our right shoulder, the diver in front of me suddenly jumped and pulled his arms up. I saw an eye and a lime green head disappearing into a hole in the reef. I later learned that a moray eel had seen the flash of his silver watch. When the head of the eel darted out of the hole, the diver reacted. It's lucky the diver had good reflexes, or he would have had a huge hole in his arm from those teeth and maybe no watch.

We had an afternoon off. We walked downtown after lunch to do some shopping. Beth knew the best stores. I found souvenirs reflecting the Dutch who inhabit Bonaire. I bought a Delft silver bracelet with a dime sized stone. I also purchased Delft blue hand embroidered bureau scarfs and tablecloths that would make perfect gifts.

While walking along the sidewalk, a bulletin board caught my eye. The annual swim to Klein Bonaire was held while we were visiting. Klein Bonaire is a two-mile square island a half mile off the coast of Bonaire. I found another diver who was interested in entering with me. No way Beth was going.

How exciting to swim in the open ocean. When Gwen and I arrived, we had magic marker numbers painted on our upper arm. The whole town was there, kids and elderly alike, some even using walkers to enter the water. Gwen and I lined up on the shore, flippers and masks in our hands, and the starting shot went off.

We entered the water in the midst and frenzy of the participants. It would be a half mile in the open ocean. As I began, I could see the ocean floor. As I kicked, I made slow progress and kept looking up to make sure I was with the group and going straight ahead. I lost Gwen. Soon there was no ocean floor, just water getting darker. It felt like I had been out here a long time. Often, I would pop my head up and look through my goggles. I was reassuring myself that I was with the group and nearing the opposite shore.

Private boats had volunteered to take the swimmers back to the main island. I couldn't believe that I just swam a half mile in open water. Tired but still excited, I found a boat that offered an arm to hoist me up. Not gracefully, I rolled into the boat, scraping my leg along the wood, but thankful for the ride back. I found Gwen on the beach. She had turned back when she couldn't see the ocean bottom. That evening, I had an adventure to share with Beth.

Bonaire is a sanctuary for not only flamingos but also for donkeys. Donkeys roam everywhere like dogs. The island is very flat, barely above sea level, which traps ponds of sea water. Salt flats are numerous, and salt is mined here. Wanting to explore other sections of the island, we accepted a trip from friends. Our group rented several trucks to take a trip to area known for great dives from the shore.

Four-wheel drive trucks were necessary as the roads had deep holes. Air in this desert environment was so hot it took my breath away. We saw groups of donkeys and cactus trees along the flat desert. It was too desolate for human habitation.

At the dive site, we had to carry our equipment to the water and walk in over the coral reef. Once in, the diving was fantastic. Beth and I floated along at sixty feet when she pointed to a couple of lobsters having a sword fight with their long antennae. Lobsters here are purple and have no pinchers. Entranced, we followed the battle along the ocean bottom. Not paying attention to our depth, I was shocked when I looked at my gauge. We were at eighty feet. Hating to leave such an underwater event, we made our way back to our group. The champion of the lobster battle will forever be unknown.

As we began our ascent, I was last in line to get on the boat. One more glance in the clear water through my mask, I spied a giant green moray eel, slithering along the bottom at about twenty feet. He must have been fifteen feet long and as wide around as my body. I yelled, "Hey, there's a giant moray down there!"

Divers jumped from the boat into the ocean with snorkel masks. Floating on the surface while the eel was unaware of the interest from above, we watched as he made his way out of view. We reluctantly reboarded. We all agreed that seeing this creature from above was better than meeting it face to face.

Tomorrow was departure day and it felt like we just arrived. Beth and I wondered where we would be going next year.

# CHAPTER 15 PUERTO RICO DIVE TRIP

2001

Finishing charts at the urgent care clinic, I glanced at the calendar and realized that Christmas was approaching. I would be alone for the cold South Carolina holidays. I craved warmth and a relaxed location especially after walking my dogs this morning in a forty-degree headwind. Destiny intervened. A few days later, I checked my mailbox and found a dive magazine advertising a week-long dive trip to Puerto Rico over Christmas week.

Nexton Diving Cruises are live-aboard trips for scuba diving. The giant white ship resembled an overgrown catamaran. It had two massive pontoons to stabilize the boat. The large upper deck had a jacuzzi. The rooms were private with air conditioning and a shower. World class meals were served. The dive staff were certified, and dives planned for ease and enjoyment. Most important was the tropical weather. I called the next morning to make sure there was still room for me. Yes, I'll be wearing my bathing suit and flippers for Christmas.

Friends asked me, "Jeanne, aren't you scared to be traveling alone?" My reply was, "Well, when I get off the plane and go to the assigned area, all my new friends will be there waiting for the same bus to the ship." Simple.

After taking my equipment to the dive shop for inspection, I checked to make sure that my scuba diving certification card and my passport were current. I have my plane ticket. Now to shop for decent bathing suits in the middle of winter. Fortunately, Myrtle Beach is a tourist destination, and I found a local store with a large selection.

Soon, my duffel bag was packed with bulky dive equipment. This trip my luggage will be my duffel bag and a knapsack. Shorts, tops, flip flops and odds and ends would be packed in the dive bag. My camera, medications, paperbacks, and sundries would be in my knapsack.

The plane trip from South Carolina to Puerto Rico was short. After arriving at the airport, even with no sense of direction, I found the meeting site easily. There were nine travelers. After introductions and excited conversation about our upcoming dives, the bus arrived. We were ship bound.

The boat was much larger than it appeared in the picture. Even though it was cold at home when I left, it was a pleasant eighty degrees when I arrived. Fifteen eager divers gathered on the upper deck. We were introduced to the staff and enjoyed a video presentation of our trip around the islands and reefs where we would be diving.

My room had a large square wooden frame with a mattress inside. It was placed to avoid any rolling waves from the catamaran pontoons. There was an adjoining bathroom with shower. I unpacked my clothes and made my way to the meeting room to visit and get a cold drink.

As soon as the ship left port, the migraine began. I thought my head would explode. That was followed by leaning over the side of the ship with sea sickness. The super-duper pontoons that were advertised as a smooth ride weren't working. I rarely get seasick.

I took a Dramamine and two Excedrin migraine. A sympathetic cook made me some toast. With my Gatorade in hand, I retired early. I was sick all night. In the morning, one of the divers came into my room to check the placement of my bed. He discovered that my bed was facing the wrong direction causing me to feel the rolling of the ship. My mattress was realigned, and I hoped that night would be better.

Not improving my first day at sea, and taking more medicine, I buddied up with Sarah for the first morning dive. I was dry heaving while putting on my equipment. Sarah kept whispering, "We'll be in the water soon, Jeanne. You'll feel better."

Anchoring at our first dive site off a bare rocky cliff, the water was breaking in swells against the metal stairwell we used to enter the water. The stairs rose about six to eight feet, then crashed down into the water. I looked at Sarah. "Can you believe that we have to time our entrance into the water in these waves?"

She rolled her eyes and stepped ahead of me. "I'll enter first. Watching me might help." Sarah was so helpful, and I could not have had a better buddy dive partner. A recent widow, she had no children and thought it would be nice to get away during the holidays.

With the assistance of three dive attendants, all the divers entered the water without a problem. After not diving for a couple of years, it was a rough entrance to reach the group below. I wasn't wearing enough weight around my waist and my butt wanted to bob to the surface.

Sarah was right. Being underwater relieved my nausea. I could deal with the lingering headache. The coral reef was alive with colors and fish. The purple sea fans were waving with the underwater drifts. Yellow brain corals the size of cars were surrounded by clown fish and a colorful variety of vegetation. We followed the ocean floor to the edge of a canyon. At sixty feet, I hoped that we were not going deeper into the abyss. The dive master pointed out a local resident octopus and a small cave housing a green turtle. I was relieved when the group turned back toward the ship.

After the dive, I had lunch and relaxed on the deck in the sunshine, enjoying the company of other divers. One diver had a professional camera, and we watched his pictures of us on our first dive. By the time we met as a group for the discussion about our next dive, my nausea and headache were back. The captain offered me some of his Bonine tablets. I thanked him for being so generous and found within a couple of hours, my symptoms were much relieved.

The winter season here is usually mild, but this week the seas have been rough. Envision a set of metal steps rising and dropping into a rough surf. You're in the water with a heavy tank on your back, flippers on your feet. You must put flippers in your right hand, find a metal step with your bare foot, reach up at the precise moment to the dive assistant on the boat with your left hand, and prepare to be airlifted to the top of the stairs. If you miss, you're back into rough water with no flippers on your feet.

My stomach was growling but I was afraid to eat. Their Gatorade tasted like medicine. I had a sandwich at supper. Just as I drifted off to sleep, I heard a loud thud, then footsteps running on the deck above me. I recalled we were anchored off a large cliff and the surf was rough. Wondering if we were going to crash into the cliff, I grabbed my life jacket and put it on. Should I go abovedeck?

Curiosity got the best of me. I slipped into the hallway, hanging on to keep from being thrown sided to side. An unsteady guy in shorts outside my door said, "The rope snapped off the anchor. They have it retied." I smiled to myself as I noticed he also was barefoot and his life jacket on. Enough excitement for tonight. I headed back to bed and hopefully some sleep.

The dives were spectacular as we traveled from island to island. Being underwater was such a relief. The nausea had subsided somewhat, and it was just the headaches to control.

The dive the next morning was reported to be one of the best of the week. It would be a cave dive.

Sarah and I helped each other into our equipment and made our way to the back of the ship to the stairs. Miraculously, the sea was calm today. The sea gulls were noisily diving for fish. A nearby small island was alive with birds of all types. My guess was that the caves were under this island. Maybe used by pirates?

We met our dive master at seventy feet. The sea floor was flat and devoid of corals. A few fish meandered around looking for breakfast and avoiding us. We followed the dive master closely. I knew we were going deeper without looking at my depth gauge because my ears were popping. When I looked, the gauge indicated ninety feet. I glanced over at Sarah, and she shrugged her shoulders. I wondered if she was as afraid as I was.

As we discussed prior to the dive, we would follow the diver ahead of us until we were through the cave. There would be no backing up, just going forward. I was having second thoughts, but it was too late as we entered the cave. No sunlight. Disturbed sand caused visibility problems.

Following the fins ahead of me through the murky water, I felt the tank on my back hit rock above me. When I exhaled, my belly hit the sandy bottom. I breathed in and out as fast as I could and kept kicking. I kept reminding myself, don't lose sight of the fins in front of you. Relief does not describe my feeling when I reached open water.

Christmas morning, a dive was planned in the harbor of Boquerón, a small island southwest of Puerto Rico. In the afternoon we would be on solid ground for Christmas dinner.

We wore our Christmas hats underwater while our resident photographer took our pictures. We explored the harbor bottom at a shallow depth for about thirty minutes. Compared to most of our other dives it was a nice relaxing dive as the sea was calm. We were all anxious to get dressed, enjoy the ground under our feet, and have Christmas dinner together.

Boquerón was alive with Christmas music, decorations, and crowds of locals in the streets. All the small shops and restaurants were open. We selected an outdoor patio with twinkling Christmas lights. The onshore breeze was warm, and we were happy to be on solid ground, celebrating the holiday. One more night on the ship and we would be making port tomorrow morning.

My trip was worth every minute spent underwater in Puerto Rico. I plan to be warm next Christmas. I wonder where that will be?

# CHAPTER 16
# GALAPAGOS ISLANDS

2012

I am rewarding myself with a dream vacation. After working as a registered nurse and a physician assistant for the past fifty-two years, I am retiring at the age of seventy. Ready for the next phase of my life.

All my friends take cruises and rave about them. Being on a ship with thousands of people, eating around the clock, and spending a few hours visiting an island sounds boring. My idea of fun is flying to that island, renting a car, exploring, and meeting local people.

I received a National Geographic magazine along with other brochures to check out exotic vacation spots all over the world. As I read about the National Geographic ships and their destinations, I found what I was looking for. I could fly to Ecuador, stay overnight, then on to the Galapagos Islands for a ten-day voyage on the National Geographic ship, Endeavor, with less than a hundred passengers. This was my dream trip.

Why the Galapagos? The alternative was Bora Bora and Tahiti. A friend advised me to choose the Galapagos Islands because they are fragile and changing with time and visitors. Bora Bora will always be there to visit later.

I've seen every movie about Galapagos, my favorite being, *MASTER AND COMMANDER* with Russell Crowe. I read Darwin's *Origin of the Species* in my teens when I was questioning religion and natural selection. The concept opened my eyes to expanding my mind and scientific concepts.

Darwin's five-week trip in 1835 to Galapagos was as a passenger on the HMS Beagle. He received his scientific training at two universities in Great Britain and was selected for the voyage as one of the most respected scientists of his time. On his trip, he visited six of the thirteen islands. The zoological and botanical notes he kept assisted him in later years to arrive at his natural selection theories that rattled the world.

My ship, the Endeavor, would be waiting for me off the coast of Ecuador, welcoming me aboard on January 11, 2013.

I drove to Miami from Myrtle Beach and stayed overnight because I had an early flight in the morning. The flight from Miami to Guayaquil, Ecuador would take four hours.

Paying for a single room on the ship was way over my budget so I would have a roommate. I had to pack light since I was sharing a small room. This trip involved hiking excursions, so shorts, T-shirts, and sneakers were all I needed. No dressing up for meals. I checked one suitcase and packed a carry on with suntan lotions, hats, sweatshirt, camera, film, etc. My passport carrier that I wear inside my shirt also contained extra money. I put a copy of my passport and a couple of twenties in a tiny silk purse, pinned inside my bra (a suggestion from my mother).

I took two semesters of Spanish in college, but I needed a refresher. I compiled pages of needed phrases, and useful sentences like where is the bathroom and where do I find a cab. After my trip to Mexico with my friend Kay, I remembered how to order a cold beer.

As soon as I slid into my window seat, a couple stopped in the aisle and smiled at me. The woman said something in Spanish. So much for all my studying. I smiled and said, *no comprende.* They organized their items under the seat, and we all buckled in. That ended any further conversation.

My ears began popping as the plane descended. Knowing that we would be flying over Quito, Ecuador, I watched for the high mesas. Majestic mountains with flat tops appeared like they magically arose from the earth. Some were bare and others had villages laid out in neat squares like children's colorful blocks.

My destination city of Guayaquil appeared below the cloud cover, tiny cars, church spires, and hills in every direction with miniature houses stuck to the steep slopes.

Following our plane group to the baggage claim area, I waited as the belt went round and round, until there were no more suitcases. I saw a small office and asked about lost luggage A polite clerk gave me a form to fill out with my name and hotel. Thank goodness I usually put a couple of days of clothing in my carry-on.

I was concerned that my group had left but when I found the bus arrival area, I sighed with relief. I saw a sign with the name of my ship, The Endeavor. The driver had returned for any late arrivals. He was so polite and concerned about my lost luggage. He took me to the hotel and introduced me to the crew leader of our group. Ramon was super attentive and filled out paperwork for me. He called the hotel taxi to take me to the nearby mall to pick up any items I would need. As I was leaving, he said, "Miss Gates. Your taxi will wait for you outside the door of the mall. Do not get into any other taxi." That made me a little nervous.

As my taxi pulled into the mall entrance, there was a man on either side of the door with a machine gun. I'm not a gun expert, but those weapons sure frightened me. I found a store that looked like The Gap. The young clerk and I laughed all the way through our conversation. I tried telling her my luggage was *perdu avion* and made an airplane with my hand. After finding a couple of tops and shorts that would look better on my granddaughter, I pointed to my bra strap. With a wide smile, she pointed down the mall, telling me *cinco derecho,* which meant nothing to me until I found the lingerie shop.

My taxi was waiting at the door as I exited, apparently paid for by the hotel as he just smiled and dropped me off at the hotel entrance. I smiled at Ramon as I entered the lobby. The Endeavor group was convened at the far end of the lobby, enjoying drinks and snacks. I'm not good at entering a room of strangers and socializing. There was a group of four women who were chatting and laughing, so I joined them. Great choice. They included a paramedic, a nurse anesthetist, a judge, and a businesswoman. I knew we would be good friends this trip.

There was an announcement that all the passengers meet at the marina for our trip to the ship. I wasn't prepared to be taken on a Kodiak. Twelve passengers at a time boarded, stepping into a rubber bottomed boat with inflated sides. We held on to ropes while we were ferried to the ship offshore. These boats would be our transportation to and from the islands during our trip. I was starting to relax and have fun.

The ship was far ahead in the open sea, looking every bit as impressive as it appeared in the brochure. As I watched it gently wobble on the water, I was anxious to be on board and start my adventure.

I made my reservation on the ship early, so I had a choice of rooms. I was on the upper deck. After my sea sickness last year on a catamaran dive trip, I hoped being up high would be a smoother ride. The ship was large and seaworthy, and when I boarded, there was only a gently rolling motion, as small waves made smacking sounds against the hull.

At sunset, we were introduced to the captain and crew in the lounge. Drinks and snacks were served by a friendly and attentive staff. Our luggage was delivered to our rooms during the meeting, minus mine! Practical information about the ship and insights into our tours were reviewed. After a mandatory boat drill, we were invited to a buffet lunch. During the lunch, the ship would be sailing to Santa Cruz, a nearby island. After settling into our cabins and a rest, the Zodiacs would take us to explore our first Galapagos Island.

My room was small and had a bathroom with shower. There was a note on my small desk that my roommate had cancelled. Looking around, I was relieved. I could not imagine rooming with a stranger in such small quarters. My carry-on bag was on my bed. Not much to unpack. I overheard a conversation that mine was not the only luggage lost.

There were sixty-five passengers on this expedition. The staff numbers were about half that. Everyone met in the lounge and split up into groups of ten or twelve. Our expedition leader, Raul, briefed us on the National Park rules, the most important one: Never touch any wildlife. They are not afraid of humans. If you touch a turtle, you will be sent home and barred from ever returning.

Our group boarded, excited to see marine iguanas and flamingos. Each Kodiak had a naturalist, ours today was Gilda. Swirling my hand in the ice-cold water, I leaned over to find that I could see at least thirty feet in clear sea water. We landed on a flat, wide, sandy beach called Las Bachas. As the group gathered around Gilda, she led us up a trail of well-traveled lava with low thorny bushes on each side. As she explained the wildlife, it was evident that her life was devoted to protecting the islands.

We hadn't walked more than a half mile when our route was blocked by a giant tortoise, just lumbering along showing no sense of fear. Its shell was immense in proportion to a tiny head and feet. Stepping around him or her, there were lots more ahead. A Galapagos brown speckled hawk looked down at us from a high branch. We encountered a small fresh-water pond where bright pink flamingos fed in the distance. Their color is derived from the shrimp they eat. There were many birds on this island, some here that may not be seen on any other of the islands. A shoreline on the way back was inhabited by hundreds of marine iguanas. Really ugly creatures. It was necessary to step over them. I got too close and one hissed loudly. At least it didn't bite.

When we returned to our beach, Gilda pointed out marks in the sand. East Pacific green sea turtles come up on the beach at night to nest. She said if we watch, we can see their heads in the water while mating. Mating can last hours. That got a few raised eyebrows.

Returning to the ship, I was tired but anxious to attend the welcome aboard cocktail party, where the ship's officers and natural history staff will be formally presented. I was not aware that this voyage had National Geographic photographers among the guests. They would assist with cameras and techniques, and seminars. I also had a pleasant surprise. My lost luggage was sitting on my bed!

I was impressed with the knowledge of the captain and his staff. We were reminded that we are visiting an extremely fragile environment and one of the most strictly protected national parks in the world. A zero impact was encouraged.

The buffet dinner was an elegant affair. Waiters who we would see daily were friendly and attentive. A large selection of beer and wine was available. My white wine was delicious and appreciated after a long day. If this was the buffet, I could only imagine the regular meals. Several choices of hot or cold soups, sandwich meats, cheeses, home-made breads, a wide variety of fruit and a dessert cart to die for. I wouldn't be going to bed hungry tonight. Seating was random, and I met some remarkably interesting people. Tomorrow we'll be visiting North Seymour and Rabida Islands.

As we settled in our Zodiac, Jonathan introduced himself as our naturalist for   today. He was tall with satiny black hair falling on his uniform collar, nice biceps, and a killer smile. I'll try to pay attention to the birds. We're on North Seymour Island for a loop walk on a well-traveled path that takes us to a wide open, and uneven, rocky meadow. He pointed out a pair of blue footed boobies. They were shuffling their feet, necks gyrating up and down, feathers puffing out, and circling each other like a bullfighter and bull. It was their mating dance. Four males who seemed interested, watched from a distance. One decided to "break in" but was immediately chased away. Nature had staged this spectacle for us today. As we moved on, we had lots of opportunities for pictures. Male frigate birds with swollen red chests were wooing mates.

Back at the beach we watched sea lions and small lizards scooting about at the ocean's edge. I'm amazed that none of these animals are in the least frightened by the attention. Our Kodiak ride back to the ship was always refreshing. Everyone was chatting about what they saw and pictures they couldn't wait to see.

After lunch, the National Geographic photographers were holding a camera session. My camera was a point and shoot. I also had an I-pad that had a big screen and took excellent pictures. I changed into my bathing suit for the afternoon snorkeling off Rabida Island.

On the way to Rabida, Jonathan told us about eradication of rats and goats from this island to balance the delicate ecosystem. A striking red beach is due to a high iron oxide content in the lava. Jonathan led us to the end of a beach where the water was deep.

Entering the water was painful. The currents through the Galapagos islands bring cold water. Today the water was seventy degrees. My interest in the fish below was the only reason I snorkeled for twenty minutes. I spied a sea lion, so graceful underwater. A manta ray slid along the ocean floor. Best of all, a black starfish with red dots. Our group stayed on the beach for photos of sea lions galloping and playing up and down the beach.

We all met in the lounge later for a short lecture about sea lions. Then off to another memorable five-star dinner with wine.

After a quick shower, I was sound asleep within minutes, lulled to sleep by the gentle hum of the engines.

In the morning, we traveled north, past the island of Isabela, also called Albemarle. Today our naturalist is Giancarlo. A college professor type, also handsome. The frigid sea water in this area of fifty degrees can cause thick fogs. Due to the cold water, there was a rich marine ecosystem attracting whales and dolphins. As we approached Fernandina Island, there was an imposing 5000-foot volcano, one of the most active volcanos in the world. The stark coastline was inhabited by marine iguanas.

As our Kodiaks tied up at a wooden pier, we stepped out onto a beach of lava and sand. Iguanas were everywhere. We stepped around them as they hissed at the interruption. It was obviously mating season. As we continued inland, we saw flightless cormorants, herons, sea lions, and even some penguins. I never expected to see penguins here.

Next, we traveled by Zodiac to Isabela Island. A volcano had collapsed here, leaving a great view of the inner caldera. Traveling on the water around the island, at the base of tall cliffs, we had great photo opportunities. There were more cute penguins, cormorants, and turtles swimming in the bay. Isabela has five volcanos, one of which is the highest point of all the islands.

Since the eradication of goats on this island, native inhabitants that once faced extinction are recovering. Darwin spent time here and a lake bears his name. Several members of our group climbed steep stairs that went up forever to visit the lake. I opted to stay below and watch the turtles and diving birds as the light gradually faded into pink skies.

At sunset tonight, the big event was a cocktail party on the deck to celebrate crossing the equator. Our group of girls who had been experiencing this saga together, gathered at the railing, drinks in hand, and raised our glasses as we passed twin rocks jutting from the ocean at the equator. We then enjoyed a festive dinner. After dinner, we hastily found a good seat in the lounge for a presentation on Darwin.

Right after breakfast the next morning, an announcement was made over the PA system that the sea was flat, and we could possibly see turtles and whales. Several of us watched huge sea turtles, heads above the water, some mating, but no whales were spotted.

Today, the entire group on board spent the day on Santiago Island. We took a bus to a turtle "farm". Huge verdant pastures with a large muddy pond were inhabited by hundreds of land tortoises, most of them about five years old. They extended their long necks reaching yellow hibiscus bushes, cotton plants and yellow and white flowers with a pea-like berry. The temperature was rising, and several tortoises were milling around in the mud.

After lunch at a local outdoor restaurant, our guides took us inland to a lovely shoreline walk where they pointed out many local birds where we sighted another brown Galapagos hawk. We even saw a small colony of fur seals in deeply carved grottos along the cliffs. Darwin spent nine of his nineteen days on this island.

On the way back to the ship in our Zodiac, the sea was calm, and it was quiet. A small penguin swam by as two cormorants buzzed us while fishing. Suddenly two humpback whales surfaced close to us. Our guide estimated then to be over sixty feet in length. As the sky became pinker, we followed them out to sea until we were far from the ship and had to turn around.

My favorite part of this trip was a day on Santa Cruz Island, the largest island of the chain. I explored a quaint small town with bright pastel-colored shops along the streets. As we walked toward the harbor in town, sea lions occupied the park benches. Several small boats were tied up at the pier, and fisherman were in the process of cutting up fish to sell.

A man wearing a black apron was slicing fish as a massive sea lion sat on his feet, barking at him, and clapping his flippers, begging for a piece of fish. The man tossed a morsel from his knife into the air, and the sea lion caught it easily, barking and clapping for more. Penguins and iguana also lined the ledges nearby hoping for handouts.

I found some interesting weavings in one shop. I weave on a small loom at home, and I found these weavings intricate and colorful. Jewelry and original artwork along with metal sculptures captured everyone's attention.

A bus ride away was a local hacienda in a mountainous part of the island. The air was fragrant from the acres of fruit trees nearby. They served lunch on long tables on an open porch. We started with a local vegetable soup, followed by steamed fish and yellow rice. The dessert was a warm bread pudding with coconut. Yummy.

The highlight of the trip was a visit to the Darwin Center. The famous turtle, Lonesome George, had died last year and was replaced by a turtle from the San Diego Zoo named Diego. George had fathered many offspring and it was now Diego's job.

For many years in the past, local conservationists have protected the tortoise. When the numbers began to decline, they collected eggs and incubated them in sheds. They used lightbulbs and donated hair dryers from tourists to control the temperature in their outdated buildings. Eventually, the sheds became modern as they are today.

I learned some very interesting facts about tortoises. Eggs buried deep in the sand that is cooler become males. Those eggs warmer at the top layer become females. A blood test is needed to determine the sex.

We toured the center for hours, and I was amazed at the number and sizes of tortoises there. If they had left me there for another week, I would have been happy. If I were much younger,

I might have considered living in Santa Cruz and joining in the conservation effort in Galapagos Islands.

Today would be our last day. We would spend the day on San Cristobal Island. As our Zodiac tied up on a flat sandy beach flanked on each side by tall cliffs, we dropped our bags along the beach, preparing to break up into groups for an island hike.

Sea lions began arriving as if they had been waiting for us. A mother and a pup walked up to a photographer, without fear and close enough to pet. The pup spied something far down the beach and was off and running. We all began taking pictures of him. He barked and ran, and when he got to his destination, it was a knapsack on the sand. He circled it barking, lost interest, and ran back up the beach to his mother.

We traveled up a dry stream bed to a landscape like a southwest desert. It was a volcanic moonscape with red flowered cacti. The view from the cliff on the summit was worth the hike. We could see in all directions, a blue cloudless sky, countless sea and island birds in flight, and there was our ship.

On the way down the rocky trail, I glanced over into some rocks and saw a small, scrawny tiger cat that ran away quickly. Cats, dogs, pigs, goats, and other animals not indigenous to these islands have systematically been removed. Guess that cat was using his nine lives.

Our fantastic five girls sat together at the captain's champagne dinner that night. We toasted to our storybook trip. Most of our table ordered filet that we didn't need a knife to cut. The champagne was smooth and the company unsurpassed.

I awoke with a start at five a.m., hoping I had not overslept. I showered and packed, as we would be leaving right after breakfast at six-thirty. At eight-fifteen we were transported to the dock to board busses to the airport. Many of us exchanged contact information to keep in touch. Two of us were on the same flight and said goodbye to our other three new friends.

Once I arrived in Miami, I picked up my car from the hotel lot and decided to drive the twelve hours to Myrtle Beach. I was anxious to return home to my pets and to embark on the new retirement phase of my life.

# CHAPTER 17
# SIENA ITALY

2013

In the fall of 2013, my friend Kathy asked me if I would like to join her for a trip to Tuscany to enjoy wine tours. The word "yes" hadn't even escaped my lips before I was mentally selecting my outfits.

Learning about wine was imperative. Ordering *THE EVERYDAY GUIDE TO WINES* from Great Courses, I finished the complete lecture series presented by a sommelier that included the lexicon of wine. While at wine tastings, I could appreciate the variety of wines and blend in with proper etiquette.

Kathy and I agreed that by staying outside the big cities and find a hotel in a small town like Siena, we could explore the area and absorb the flavor of Italy; visiting shops and restaurants would allow us to meet local people. The hotel we selected was in the center of town and had reasonable rates. We could travel to wine tasting events from a central location.

The other reason for staying in one place was that neither of us had a sense of direction. We could get lost crossing through one intersection. Siena was perfect. It is an ancient walled city with lovely shops, open air restaurants, and cobblestone streets. A walled city meant that it was enclosed, and we couldn't get lost. Right?

I over packed again, taking a large metal suitcase, a carry on and a knapsack. Kathy also found she had taken too large a suitcase with wheels that squeaked. She was a frequent flyer and flew first class while I roughed it in coach.

The flight was long, and I felt like a sardine. Lucky to be in an aisle seat, I could stretch and when standing, peek through portholes near passengers to see the crystal blue ocean below. My first glance of Italy was mountains floating by and then I felt a bump of the landing gear.

The Leonardo di Vinci International Airport in Rome was like a city. As we walked through, I was shocked to see hairdresser and barber shops, and I could even get a massage or rest in a lounge. Finding our baggage belt was like the Lewis and Clark expedition. Strange languages floated by as I strained to catch a few words.

I could have enjoyed people watching a while longer, but my luggage appeared on the belt. Kathy's bright green bags were a few suitcases later. Finding the exit was easy, and canary yellow taxis were lined up at the curb.

As our luggage was placed in the trunk, Kathy asked the driver, "Roma Termini, per favore." I was impressed and hoped she knew more of the language. As we were leaving the airport, she asked the taxi driver, in Italian, "Could you take us past the Coliseum on the way to the train station?"

He smiled back, and in a very friendly tone replied, "Si, Senora." True to his word, as slowly as traffic would allow, our taxi crept by the famous coliseum. "It still looks like the Gladiator movie. Can you believe we're here?" I whispered to Kathy..

"Yes, and I love Italy. My last trip here was two years ago with a wine group. I missed hearing Italian spoken." Kathy sighed and smiled.

"Ok, I'll let you do the talking. All I know is hello and good-bye."

Arriving at the Rome Termini Train Station, the biggest in the city, the first hurdle was to purchase train tickets to Siena. Unkempt young men and women began approaching us, asking us to let them help with the ticket machines. They were like locusts. We clutched our knapsacks to our chest, hoping they could not open any outer zippers. Meanwhile, we kept our eyes on our luggage. We later learned that these annoying people were gypsies and adept pickpockets.

"Signora, I will help. I will help. The ticket machines. I will help you and you will give me tip, Si?" This girl appeared to be a teen with intense eye contact, unmatched shoes without socks, a long blue threadbare coat, and a pushy attitude. Her two male friends were approaching Kathy to help her.

It was easier not to alienate them but allow them to help just to get rid of them. We carefully took out twenty euros to purchase the tickets. We checked the train fares before leaving home. Taking out two euros each, we gave it to them as a tip. We didn't get a smile or a thank you.

We quickly left for our train gate. At least, in the general direction we thought was our gate. Being tired and jet lagged, we were not at our best. After one hour of searching, we finally found it. Leaving Kathy guarding the luggage, I looked for a restroom. It had a turnstile and coin machine to get inside. Italian money! I backtracked into the terminal and found a store where I purchased fresh bread sandwiches with a pizza looking filling, some cookies with pink icing, two fruit drinks, and two bottles of water for the long train trip to the hotel. I also got a lot of coins for restrooms.

After using the restroom, I found Kathy exactly where I left her. She told me, "Some American travelers told me that there are pickpockets in the station and to be very careful with our luggage." Wish we had that information on the way in.

Train travel in Europe is so easy. The hard part is finding the appropriate gate. In the misty rain, we walked up and down the station's platform, searching for a SIENA sign.  After asking several passengers, one elderly Italian woman pointed us in the right direction. With drippy hair and sense of relief, we boarded the train. I asked Kathy, "I hope this is the right train. Do you remember that song about the man who rode the subway beneath the streets of Boston, the man who may never return? Good thing we have snacks."

She just laughed. "I just looked at the train schedule and we should be there in three hours." I know Kathy well and the look on her face was not reassuring.

The train was local, not an express. We stopped at small stations, sometimes a few passengers would disembark, and then we would anxiously look for the next sign. Every town had a central church, usually beautiful, ornate, appearing too big for such a tiny village.

Finally. We both breathed a big sigh of relief. SIENA. Dragging all our luggage out onto the cement platform, Kathy asked a man leaving the train, "Can you give instructions to our hotel, the Hotel Italia? He smiled and said, "No parla inglese."

She smiled her nicest smile and asked, "Hotel Italia, per favore? He pointed up. The hill was enormous. No taxis or bus in sight. Kathy, always considering her pocketbook, announced, "A taxi is too expensive for such a short ride."

"Are you kidding me? We'll have to lug our suitcases way up that hill. And once we get up there, how far to the hotel?" Tears were in my eyes, not from crying but I think I was delirious.

Kathy got laughing, crossed her legs, and suddenly cried out, "Oh my God. I think I have to pee before we try the hill." Dropping her luggage, she dashed into the terminal. I tried to be polite when I called, "Do you have some coins?"

We slowly dragged our luggage up the hill. We picked up our pace when we reached the top, spying our hotel one block away. We were both sweating so badly that the hotel clerk probably thought it was raining outside. I'm hoping for a gift of wine in my room and reclining on a soft bed.

We arrived just after lunch was served. Having just picked at our "lunch" from the Rome station, I asked Kathy, "Why don't we take a nap. We'll have dinner here at the hotel restaurant at five. We can pick up some brochures and go back to my room and make a schedule for tomorrow."

"A nap sounds like heaven. I'll meet you in the restaurant at five.  I'm glad they put us rooms in our own quiet end of the hotel." Kathy looked like exhausted as she dragged her luggage into her room.

The hotel dining room was small and comfortable. Dinner was served buffet style. There were three main selections, roast beef, white fish in a sauce, and open-faced turkey sandwich. There were also soups, salads, hot veggies and best of all, local breads that looked fresh baked and smelled scrumptious. I picked up a bowl of steaming hot vegetable soup, a small pasta salad and a large plate of bread. Why not? Nobody here knows me. Picking up several pats of butter, I found a table in a quiet corner.

When Kathy found me, her eyes big, palms up with a questioning look on her face when she saw my large plate of bread, I said, "Just sit down without making a scene. I'll share my bread".

After dinner, we ventured down the sidewalk in front of the hotel. There were many locals walking on both sides of the street. Within a few blocks, we found a pizza restaurant that looked inviting with outside tables, striped awnings with colorful lights, and laughter overpowering the conversations. A look of mutual agreement and we were inside ordering a glass of wine. The pizzas floating by on large metal pans looked and smelled heavenly. Tables were filled with mostly young people, dishes clattered, and singing could be heard from a group of young men in the back room. Kathy was eavesdropping on conversations around us and interpreting for me.

Sipping our second glass of wine, she translated. "The couple at the next table is having a fight about money. Those two guys across the aisle are discussing the girls they're taking out tonight. I wish they would talk slowly. It's been a long time since I've spoken Italian. Before my grandfather died, I could practice with him every week."

"I'm so thankful you speak Italian. When we get lost you can ask for directions." Smiling at her, I asked, "We're not going to get lost, right?"

"I'm counting on you. You're better at directions than I am. When I'm on a trip I stay in at night. But look at tonight, I'm out and having fun," Kathy remarked, turning her head as she checked out the gorgeous guy strutting by.

As we ambled back to the hotel, car traffic was light, the occasional Vesper noisily putt putting by. Several small shops along the street were closed. "Look Kathy, a small grocery store with gigantic purple grapes in baskets in the window. We're stopping by this store tomorrow."

"Ok, Jeanne, but don't wake me up early."

With a nod and smile, I knew I'd be up very early, not wasting a minute of Italy.

Early morning fog found me wandering along a narrow sidewalk. It's hard to believe that Romans could have walked this very ground as early as 27 BC. Small brick faced shops are closed but the delicious odor of fresh baked bread assaults my nostrils. I want to yell. "Wake up everybody." I wanted to see Vespas noisily zooming down the streets, locals strolling to work, and chairs and umbrellas appearing on sidewalks to welcome early morning diners.

Pounding on Kathy's door on my return, I loudly

announce, "Wake up. It's coffee time in Italy."

I hear a moaning sound from inside, and heard her slippers slide along the tiled floor. The door opened a tiny crack. "Are you crazy? It's only seven o'clock."

Not to be put off any longer, I make a deal. "If you get up now, I'll get you a cup of coffee and bring it here."

Sticking her head out a fraction, I can see that her hair is still in a state of bed head and her eyes are barely open.

Right hand as in a salute covering her eyes, she moans, "All right. I'm showering as soon as you shut the door. I'll meet you in the dining room and check for my coffee outside my door in a few minutes."

As I sat in the noisy hotel restaurant, watching strangers help themselves to a buffet breakfast, I wondered where they were from, what they did back home, were they having fun? Dishes clattered from silverware and conversation was in several languages. Soon, Kathy appeared at the doorway, eyes puffy and no makeup. At least she had combed her hair.

"I haven't been up this early in years. Thanks for the coffee you left. Did you eat yet?"

"No, I was waiting for you. Let's go see what they have." As I walked around the buffet table, I selected scrambled eggs, bacon, pastry with white frosting and a decaf coffee with cream.

Her plate contained one lonely English muffin and some jelly. She clutched a coffee, black, in her shaky hand. "I'm so tired. Don't let me fall asleep while I'm sitting here."

Ignoring her comments and bad attitude, I commenced to review the brochures, suggested today's tour of the ancient city and ravaged my breakfast.

It took Kathy another hour to get dressed, but finally we were off. We followed our hotel street, Strada di Vicobello. Why don't streets at home sound so romantic? A short walking distance revealed the reddish brick walls of the ancient city. A chill traveled up my spine when I passed under an ornate rounded portal. I was about to visit the Piazza del Compo that I saw in the movie, Quantum of Solace, when Daniel Craig ran through the horse race called the Palio held in the piazza.

The narrow streets were dwarfed by tall ancient buildings on either side. Some streets were older, with cobblestones in disarray, threatening to trip you. Other streets were a mix of flat stones or patterned bricks. Siena means orange-red color and the color of earth in this region. Probably why everywhere I looked, there were reddish bricks and houses. Shops were plentiful, lining the streets, some with inviting colorful umbrellas and tables.

We picked out a tiny restaurant on a side street to visit on the way back where we could enjoy a glass of wine served with a plate of bread, dipping olive oil with herbs and a plate of meats. First, we had to visit the Piazza del Campo.

Restaurants, tall apartments, vendors with kiosks, and an ornate church surround a giant open space with a red brick surface. Probably bigger than a couple of football fields back home. Hundreds of visitors meandered over the area with vendors in colorful flagged carts luring tourists with souvenirs. We blended in shoulder to shoulder with the crowd, soaking up the excitement of the moment, mouths open, heads up, like those around us.

Anytime is wine time in Italy. Finding a small table under an umbrella, ordering a glass of wine from a cute waiter, we sat back, looked at each other and said, "Vito Bella!" We toasted our first glass and sat back, enjoying the ambiance of Italy.

There were the most handsome Italian men strutting by. I grabbed my camera and took some shots. I had to prove to our girlfriends back home just how incredibly handsome all the men were. We agreed that the women here were also beautiful. In the back of my mind, I was wondering if I could live in Italy on my social security check.

We perused the shops, bought some T-shirts from the vendors and on our way home, stopped at that cute restaurant for wine. Dipping the fresh bread into the green olive oil with herbs, we sampled the meat dish. I discovered that I love prosciutto. After a few glasses of wine, it was after four and time for a siesta. The hotel clerk recommended a nice restaurant for tonight. Finding out way home was easy even without breadcrumbs.

At seven, refreshed, we retraced our steps into the city and found our restaurant. Strings of lights over the entrance and music invited us into the darkened interior where we were seated by a waiter in a tux, white towel over his arm. It was all uphill from there. Kathy, being an expert in wines, ordered our wine, and our dinner in Italian. I was so impressed with her finesse. She had a veal dish, and I had my favorite, eggplant. The meal was so delicious that we never spoke a word until the last piece of spaghetti disappeared through our lips.

Next was dessert. It was a unanimous choice - Cannoli. Etiquette or not, I picked mine up and attacked the sweet innards. I know what I'll be ordering for dessert while I'm in Italy. There was no wine left over.

Wine tours were why we were here. On the second day, our first bus tour took us to a nearby winery. The fields in the distance were a weaving of green rows of vines. It appeared so lush, and the smooth green fields were broken by red and beige homes tucked into the hillsides. At home we would call them mansions. Fields of sunflowers were in bloom wherever we traveled.

The winery had a weathered wood exterior. On entering, the owner greeted us at the door. An elderly man with a fringe of white hair peeking out from under a cap greeted our tour group. He was dressed in baggy black pants held up with suspenders, a red print shirt topped off at the neck with a blue bowtie. He looked like he dressed in the dark but introduced himself as the owner of the winery for over fifty years. He gave the aura of a content man.

Our entire bus group was standing waiting for his tour to begin but his eyes settled on Kathy. As he started his tour, he slid her arm under his, said something like "Bella" and proceeded to give the tour. If he had been about forty years younger, she may never have left that winery.

When we planned our day trips from the brochures, we found that the Banfi Winery was a three-hour drive away from Siena. Kathy had been given a complementary day tour and lunch from a wine distributor friend. It included a tour of the entire wine making process starting at the vineyard, a five-course lunch with Banfi wines, a factory tour, and a visit to the owner's castle. We agreed that it was worth hiring a taxi and paying $350 for the trip. The price included the driver waiting for us all day and driving us back to our hotel.

Just meeting and admiring the taxi driver was worth it for me. I was double checking how I could stretch my social security income here. I saved his card. We haven't reached the winery yet, and I'm so content.

Although our driver's good looks are distracting, we were passing through breathtaking Tuscany, as perfect as a calendar picture. Green carpeted hillsides were smooth as velvet, beige homes with salmon-colored roofs were tucked away in the folds. Miles of winding rows of vines surrounded some of the estates. Sunflowers waved their happy faces everywhere.

Some wooded areas reminded me of New England, but that's only temporary as the Tuscan vistas and olive tree orchards appear. I had never seen an olive grow and couldn't wait to get up close to check it out.

Our driver has been pointing out some local wineries and told us about their special wines. Soon, we saw a dirt road with a sign, BANFI WINERY. We spotted the castle up on the hill nestled between smooth green moguls. It could be a fairy castle on the cover of a children's book.

Kathy read from the brochure. "The owners are Americans who purchased the winery in the early 1900s and are the fourth owners in five hundred years. We'll be getting a tour of the castle later today. Can you imagine waking up and surveying this beauty from your bedroom balcony every morning?"

Wistfully, I replied, "Yes, I can picture myself in a red silk bathrobe, glass of wine in hand, wind blowing my hair," at which point I said, "Dream on."

As we entered the conference center, there were distributers milling about. We visited the gift shop and helped ourselves to cookies and coffee. Kathy had promised her distributer friend to collect information for her from the company. We had a short introduction to our schedule, and we were off in golf carts to see the vines.

Winding our way up and down rows of maturing grapes, the guide pointed out the soil and how it affected the taste of the wine. A small cart whizzed by with freshly picked clusters of wine were piled to overflowing, headed for the processing area.

We stopped for a wine tasting. I was glad I had taken the course. Not being a fan of red wine, Kathy happily took care of all my samples. I found out there was one red wine I liked, the reserve. It's the first wine processed, smooth, tasty and the most expensive. Of course.

The factory was next. Huge storage vats were connected to multiple tubes and gauges, watching the ingredients carefully. Finally, the wine is placed in barrels in the basement. Huge wood barrels were lined up by the hundreds. The area was bigger than a football field.

Finally, off to the factory where 90,000 bottles of wine a day are packaged. Boxes are placed on pallets then wound with saran wrap.

We had worked up an appetite. We were looking forward to our five-course lunch.

The menu was in Italian. In English it was vegetable soup with bread, homemade pasta with beef ragout, beef and roast potatoes, and dessert with red fruit sauce. Just so you enjoy the flavor of the menu in Italian, Carpaccio di Chienna con pappa al pomodoro, Chianina beef carpaccio with tomato pappa. Desert was tortino di coccolato can salsa ai frutti. Why does it sound so much better in Italian?

Each course was paired with a wine from their winery. With an added treat with lunch, the American owner came to each table to visit with guests. She was so friendly and made us feel like we were dining in her home.

The last treat was the tour of the castle. We entered from the basement, greeted by a medieval knight in full armor, lance in his chain mail glove, standing guard in the hallway. We passed rooms with wall tapestries that had to be hundreds of years old. Plush furniture and thick carpeting reflected how wealthy these tenants were for the times.

"Darn!" said Kathy. I wanted to see my bedroom with the view."

Our driver was waiting for us. It felt good to sit still and relax after a busy day. We chatted with Sergio on our way back to the hotel. Mamma Mia! So cute!

A one-hour bus trip was scheduled the next day for a tour to San Gemignani near Florence. Seen on our approach, it was literally built into a cliff of a high hill. Kathy looked at me, arched her eye rows and said, "I don't think I can climb up those cobblestone hills. I'd have to be part mountain goat."

This village was centuries old, small stores lining the narrow cobblestone streets. Kathy and I found heirloom linens for gifts. Thankfully, there were flat areas where we caught our breath and lunched on delicious vegetable soup and homemade bread.

On our walk back to the bus, we passed a stone wall overlooking a field with trees. I was so excited. I saw olives growing on a tree, just hanging there like little green apples. It looked much bigger than the olives in a jar I use at home. It must take a lot of these to make olive oil.

That night after our tour, we walked from our hotel and strolled along the street in front of the hotel. A man was sweeping the sidewalk in front of a small restaurant. He smiled and invited us in for something to eat. We were glad we stopped.

We enjoyed the best spaghetti with tasty thick sauce, meatballs, and a glass of chianti. He sat with us, asking about our families and we asked about his. A special visit. We felt like part of the town.

We were tourists again in the ancient city the next day, shopping. I found a leather purse I couldn't live without. Didn't even ask the price. When was I going to be back in Italy? I just handed over my credit card and included a leather wallet for good measure. Kathy bought two pairs of leather shoes. Her credit card had cobwebs on it, and she was hesitant to hand it over to the clerk.

We visited Piazza del Compo again and sat enjoying our wine as before. A group of rugby players marched by with flags, singing loudly and oozing testosterone. After two glasses of wine, we explored some side streets and found the il Duomo Cathedral. It's been there since the twelfth century. Ken Follett must have used this church as a model in his book *PILLARS OF THE EARTH.* Checkerboard black and white bricks on a majestic cathedral looked unusual. I read in the brochure that the bricks were dark green.

The cathedral was adorned with gargoyles, frescos, and

saints on all sides and hanging from ramparts. It towered above all nearby buildings. Kathy didn't want to pay the entrance fee, but I couldn't resist. It wasn't just a tour. It was an experience. If you're not religious when you enter, you may find your soul inside this holy cathedral.

Stopping at our favorite tiny restaurant on a side street, we enjoyed wine with meats, bread, and olive oil. We were careful on our walk back to the hotel. Those cobblestone bricks can jump up and trip you.

Since this was our last night, we chose our pizza place around the corner. We sat outside, enjoying a warm breeze, at a table with a striped umbrella. Sipping our wine, we soaked in the last of the Italian ambiance. Our pepperoni pizza was delicious, the crust light brown and crunchy. There were no leftovers, wine, or pizza.

After all the wine we had enjoyed in one day, we carefully placed our wavering steps as we traveled back to the hotel along uneven brick streets.

We agreed to meet outside our rooms at six a.m. I would call Kathy at four to give her plenty of time to become fully conscious.

Being anxious about being on time, I sat in the courtyard in the darkness waiting for Kathy. I promised the sparkling stars, "I'll be back to Italy one day."

# CHAPTER 18 CHINA

2016

In the fall of 2015, our memoir class was asked to interview seventeen veterans at a local nursing home to compile their military stories. They would be bound in book form for their friends and family.

I chose John's name randomly from a list. I called to arrange the interview and he seemed anxious to talk about his military experiences.

Arriving at his apartment, John invited me into his living room. He said, "I'm real nervous about this interview. What should I say?"

He was a tall imposing man and moved about easily. He was wearing a blue Navy hat with lots of metal decorations. The apartment was tidy.

I tried to put him at ease. "If you don't mind, I'll record your story. Why don't you just tell me everything from when you enlisted until now, like you were telling a friend?"

Eagerly, he began his story while I recorded. When we were finished, we chatted for a while, sharing that we both had spent time in Guam and Saipan. When I returned in a few days with my typed copy, I read it to him since his eyesight was impaired due to diabetes. He put his hand on my shoulder, smiled, and said, "That is a great story you typed. Just like I said it."

As a child, he and his siblings were farmed out to local families for food in exchange for work. John lived with a local doctor who required him to do chores before school and into the evening, in exchange for meals and a place to stay. Ways to make money were a constant theme in his life.

John left home in Galena, Illinois in 1941, at the age of fifteen. He had a small metal suitcase and thirty-five cents in his pocket. His best friend accompanied him as they made their way across the state. Their first job, lasting only one day, was in a meat packing plant. They made their way to the Mississippi River. One opening was available to work on the barges. They flipped a coin and John won. His friend stayed behind, and they lost contact.

He gained experience on barges traveling up and down the Mississippi River and at the age of sixteen, decided to enlist in the Navy and travel the world on a Navy ship.

He found the nearest Navy enlistment center. He filled out the paperwork and soon found himself in a line for a physical. He was sixteen, five foot six and weighed one hundred and ten pounds. At the end of the line, he was given the sign-up sheet after passing the physical. "Get your parents to sign this and you're in, young man."

"Oh, that's not a problem. My mom is waiting downstairs. I'll be right back." Running down the stairs, he signed the paperwork, ran back up to the desk, handed over the paperwork, and said, "Ok. She signed it." He was now in the U.S. Navy.

He reported for basic training, liked the routine, had a warm place to sleep and lots of food. What he didn't like was authority, being told what to do and punishment. He soon learned ways around rules. If he did a terrible job, he wasn't asked to do that job again. He hated peeling potatoes. He and a friend decided to put them into a roller shredder and when they came out, they were the size of walnuts. They had a hundred pounds of potatoes reduced to small pile.

His rank was a boatswain's mate. His duties were in the

kitchen, painting, machinery repair, and other general duties on the ship. He loved being on the open ocean and traveling to new ports. After listening to stories about the many pranks he pulled, I understand why he never earned a higher rank.

His favorite duty was on the LST 969 in the Pacific theater. His ship loaded supplies from Saipan to the Marines on shore. Nets in the channel to the port prevented submarines from entering. As they pulled in, their props became caught in the nets. A sailor would have to dive down to assess the damage.

As the crew gathered on deck, the lieutenant in charge pointed at John and said, "Smith. You're always ready with a comment. Why don't you dive down there for us and assess the damage to the props?"

"Yes Sir," John replied with a salute. He handed his wallet to a friend, kicked off his shoes and dove in. He was now about one hundred and twenty pounds but too light to dive deep. Three fifty caliber shells were wrapped around his waist. He whispered to his friend, "If I pull on this rope, pull me up because that means sharks are trying to eat me."

He dropped like a stone to the sandy bottom, swam around the props on both sides and returned with the necessary information. It was a brave thing to at such a young age.

As he came up on deck one morning to start his shift, the ship was enveloped in a thick white fog. As the fog cleared, he asked the night officer on deck, "What are all those ships doing out there?"

"Those ships are there for the invasion of Iwo Jima." John told me he had never heard of that island. He took part in the invasion with the group of LSTs bringing in soldiers, trucks, and supplies to the beach. He saw a man crushed between trucks due to heavy surf. That bothered him for a long time.

He was also part of the invasion of Okinawa. Each of his WWII hats had LST 969 with the area he had been assigned and he was proud of each one.

China was his next assignment. He ferried prisoners up and down the Huang Pu River in Shanghai. Chinese prisoners were exchanged for Japanese prisoners. They were loaded like cordwood in barges while John and fellow soldiers held them at gunpoint. He celebrated his twentieth birthday while in Shanghai. He traveled to many cities in China.

While on shore leave with a friend in Shanghai, they were attacked, and both sustained severe knife wounds. Had they not been wearing their heavy pea jackets; they might have been killed. He recalled a big clock in the square and wanted to visit that same area when we went to China, probably to see if the red-light district was still there. He insisted, with one of his crooked smiles, that he never went there but his friends told him about it.

Eventually, his travels brought him to Hawaii, just days after the Japanese bombing. He said there were still ships smoking as they pulled into the harbor. He said he cried when he saw the Arizona on its side.

His tour in Hawaii was short and he was shipped stateside to Florida. He met a woman he liked on the base. She proposed, so he accepted. I really think he was a confirmed bachelor, but he explained that he hated to say no to her.

His wife was not military but worked with the Navy in human resources. They had an apartment on base and were happy. John enrolled in classes and completed his GED. Wanting to have a specialty in the Navy, he checked the bulletin board and found a class on photography, so he enrolled.

At a holiday party on base, he was approached by a friendly man in civilian clothes. Extending his hand to John, he said, "I'm Mr. Brown. I see on your uniform that you are D. Smith."

"Please call me John. The D stands for Deloss, which is

too hard to remember." John told me that Mr. Brown engaged him in conversation, asking him if he liked Florida, expressing interest in his new position in photography. The man smiled, said "Happy Holidays" and was gone.

It wasn't long before John was transferred to another base in Florida and was unhappy with his job. While in the cafeteria one day, Mr. Brown approached him. "Nice to see you again, John. How is everything going? Are you still taking photography classes?"

"Yes, sir, I love photography, but I'm a little unhappy with my job here."

"What would you say, John, if I could get you out of the Navy this afternoon, working in photography in a civilian position?"

Looking at him like he just offered him a million dollars, he answered, "Can you do that?"

Mr. Brown smiled, shook his hand, and walked away.

That afternoon, John heard, "Deloss Smith. Please report to human resources" over the PA system. Thinking he was in trouble, he was nervous. The paperwork for his release from the Navy was waiting to be signed and his paperwork to be assigned to the CIA to be completed. His apartment in Washington, D.C. would be waiting for him and his wife to move in.

John's new job was photography. Most of it was classified. He did share that if a picture was taken from 30,000 feet, after he developed it, he could read the headline of a newspaper being held by someone standing on the street.

John worked for the CIA until his retirement. He and his wife moved to South Carolina where he lost his wife shortly after moving into a new home. With failing health, he moved to an apartment in an assisted living facility where I met him.

When he reviewed my typed pages of his story, he asked,

"Will you take me back to China on a trip?"

Knowing it meant a lot to him, I answered," Yes, John. It sounds like fun." His health was fragile, but I felt with careful attention to his medications and using a wheelchair, he would be able to enjoy traveling.

The time to prepare for our trip was nearing. Obtaining a passport for John was the only time obstacle. We shopped for winter clothing since we would be traveling in January. During our shopping, we often went out to eat at our favorite restaurants. John loved to dine out.

We found that we liked to laugh and make jokes. He said he appreciated my willingness to swear on occasion. As an old Navy man, he sure could belt out some ribald jokes and language. I think he tried to shock me.

He had no family that visited and spent most of his time in his room. I invited him to my home where we watched his favorite show, Lonesome Dove. He loved the character Gus and said if he had he lived during that time, he would have been him. He laughed the loudest when Gus cut the cards, cheated, and won a "poke" from Lenora, the saloon dancer. John dreamed that when he died and woke up in the Lonesome Dove Saloon, he hoped he had a pocket full of silver dollars and a pack of cards.

In January 2016, we left for Hong Kong and Shanghai. We would retrace his steps during the war and celebrate his ninetieth birthday in Shanghai where he celebrated his twentieth birthday while in the Navy.

John wore his Guam WWII hat on the flight that day. Many people thanked him for his service, some stopped to chat.

After we were seated, the flight attendant stopped to meet John and as many others before her, she was enamored with him. Soon after she went back to the front of the plane we heard, "Ladies and Gentlemen. We have a celebrity on board today. A WWII veteran who served in 1942 and is revisiting his ports of call in Hong Kong and Shanghai. Let's all thank him for his service."

John was visibly moved to tears. As the applause continued, he stood up and bowed. He told me that the applause made him feel like a king.

The flight to Seattle was tiring for John and he was unable to walk up the steep incline to the terminal from the plane. I requested a wheelchair and we left for our Hong Kong gate. While the attendant wheeled him, I leaned down and asked John to hand me his hat. We had discussed not wearing the Navy hat in China. I also reminded him against salty language and political comments. I attempted to impress on him that we would be representing the U.S. until we got back home. He smiled at me, but I was still uneasy.

The Hong Kong airport was immense and busy. A Chinese woman approached us with a wheelchair as we arrived. With frequent head bows and smiles, she chatted in broken English for the long trip to customs. She laughed out loud when John touched the surface of the elevator and said, "This is stainless steel." The terminal looked like the Jetsons had just whizzed through. After taking a train through the terminal, we found customs. We cleared with smiles from the agents.

Our trip included a ride from the airport and a guide for the first day in both Hong Kong and Shanghai. A man holding a sign with our name approached us, introduced himself as Ricky our driver, and indicated that the car was a distance in the parking lot. The Chinese lady smiled and said, "I take" and pushed the wheelchair all the way to the car. We tipped her ten dollars.

Ricky spoke perfect English. During the thirty-minute ride, he pointed out landmarks. Many buildings were decorated with colorful lights. The Marco Polo Hotel was a welcome sight. Ricky made sure John had a wheelchair and assistance before he left. He told us that he and our guide, Lynora, would pick us up at nine in the morning.

This four-star hotel could rival any in the states. The desk clerks were welcoming and spoke English. The lobby was large, open, and the furniture inviting. Our attendant took us to our room where our luggage awaited us. We had adjoining rooms making it easier for me to monitor John. Our rooms were spacious and comfortable.

I woke John at seven thirty, had him shower while I selected his clothes and got out his medications. I packed my large handbag with my camera and snacks so we would be ready for pick up. We got breakfast in the hotel.

We were in the lobby after eating breakfast, precisely at eight fifty. True to his word, Ricky entered the lobby with a wheelchair. With him was an attractive, short woman with red hair pulled into a bun. She held out her hand to John, gave it a hearty shake and said, "Great to meet you, John. I'm Lynora and we'll be off for a fun day of sightseeing in Hong Kong." She turned to me and smiled, shaking my hand. "You must be Jeanne. Let's go have a fun day.

John and Lenora chatted all the way to our first stop, Vitoria Peak. We took a tram to the top, passing though lifting fog on the way up. We never saw the sun for the entire time in China. The smog hovers overhead, and many locals wore masks.

We could see the entire city from the peak. Lenora pointed out landmarks to John who asked many questions about what he remembered. We left the summit and went for a water taxi ride in the Aberdeen Harbor. Our taxi driver was named "Auntie" and had been operating her water taxi around the harbor for thirty years. She and Lenora were friends. Auntie paid a lot of attention to John and let him steer the taxi around fishing boats in the harbor. A big smile never left his face the whole ride.

We stopped for a snack from a convenience store. Lots of unidentified foods. Not much to choose from. Then off to an outdoor shopping area for souvenirs. John found a few silk scarfs for gifts. He was weak from walking and tripped and fell when he didn't see a stair. Fortunately, he did not have an injury. We were returned to our hotel where we said our farewells to Lenora and Ricky. Now we were on our own.

That evening we searched for a restaurant we saw in a brochure. I showed the taxi driver the ad and he took us there but left us off a distance away. We wandered into the back hallway of a building where we met a young Filipino girl who told us in English we had stumbled upon our restaurant, the Woolloomooloo Steak House.

She treated John like her grandfather, took his arm, led him to an elevator and found her manager. We were seated at a window table so John could see the lights of Hong Kong. John was mesmerized with the lights and changes over the years. That field with skyscrapers was just a field when he was there. When our delicious meal was done, the same girl found us and walked us to the corner where the taxis stopped. John repeated over and over, "That was a wonderful dinner and light show." The next morning, I used the hotel stationery to send a note to the restaurant telling them how wonderful their staff was and described our helper from the night before.

We went on a day-long bus trip to Macao the next day and visited the Macao Space Needle, 1100 feet tall. We watched people bungee jumping off the tower and walking around the narrow rim. And they paid up to fifteen hundred dollars to do it. John just shook his head. "Damned crazy people." From the top floor, John and I marveled at the view of inside communist China. There were metal fences with barbed wire to prevent people from crossing a river to Macao. Machine guns were mounted along the fence. John's comments should not be repeated.

We visited the casino district and stopped for lunch. Walking in a park near the ocean after lunch, we saw many barges piled high with dirt. Our guide told us dredging was being done to create new islands and enlarge others.

It was time to travel to Shanghai where our guide would meet us at the airport. I reminded John that we would be entering a communist country and to be on his best behavior. So far, he had been reserved.

Security at the airport was daunting, unfriendly, grabbing our passports and rudely shoving them back into our hands. When the attendant arrived to take us to our gate, he literally ran with the chair. I tipped him but wasn't concerned if I gave him too little. We were told when checking in to be right in this spot at flight time. I purchased sandwiches, and we ate at the gate, too scared to leave.

After a short flight, we passed through customs manned by unsmiling military. I collected our luggage and as we left the area, I saw John's name on a sign, held by a young girl. Yoyo was our new guide; English speaking and she greeted us warmly. She was married and had a four-year-old daughter. She chatted with John all the way to our hotel, giving us some history of the area and about her family life as a child there. I could tell that she was strictly government issue. During our flight, I reminded John not to make any adverse comments. I didn't want us to end up in a Chinese jail.

She attempted to explain to our desk clerks that we needed rooms on the same floor. They couldn't understand why we needed separate rooms and on the same floor. Once settled into our rooms, we left to find a restaurant. A hundred-dollar deposit was required to use the wheelchair from the hotel. We stopped at the first restaurant we saw and ordered spareribs and a noodle dish. Neither was edible. We spotted a bakery across the street and enjoyed custard pies, pastries, and brewed coffee. We would visit that bakery often. Tomorrow would be our first day in Shanghai. Yoyo would pick us up at nine.

John was excited to start his first day in Shanghai. To save his strength, I brought breakfast to his room. "I'm going to see the clock in the square today. I hope it's still there. I used to check that clock every morning before I started up the Huang Pu River with prisoners."

I had heard this comment at least a hundred times before we left, and it was a treat to see how excited he was to be here at last.

Yoyo greeted us in the lobby. A polite and sweet girl, very attentive to John. Of course, he loved that. Smiling, she asked John, Are you ready for a big day?"

"Are we going to see the clock in the square today? "

Yoyo answered, "Yes. It's our first stop."

This young lady was a gem. She guided John around in his wheelchair with ease, laughing and full of energy. First stop, downtown Shanghai. The clock tower in the square was still there as well as several old buildings. And yes, the side street John recalled as the red-light district was still there but now occupied by small stores. He shot me a glance and a smile.

Many pictures of John standing in front of the clock were taken. He indicated the location of the ramp he used to load up prisoners. Back to our car and we traveled to a city park.

There were many visitors even though it was a weekday. The paved path was lined with engraved metal memorial plaques carved with scenes of battles. Figures of lions and buddhas were placed near benches and low-lying tended bushes. The ponds were ornately designed with bridges. I took many amazing pictures.

A smoothie stand served us the worst tasting cold substance. Neither of us took more than one sample sip. Yoyo took us to a restaurant serving Dim Sum. As the lazy Susan came around, we selected noodles, a dumpling and soup. I didn't dare look or speak to John as we were under observation from other patrons. I looked at him, smiled and said, "Good, huh?"

Thank goodness he got the message and said, "Yes, very good."

I don't think we fooled Yoyo, but she was too polite to say anything. A silk factory was our next visit. Through large glass windows, we saw all stages of silkworm growth. The silk clothing in their store was sensuous and luxuriant. The prices were out of my range, but John purchased several silk purses for the girls in the offices of his many physicians.

Across the road was the museum where Yoyo dropped us off for a few hours. It was so large we decided on three floors: Chinese clothing, furniture, and money. We thoroughly enjoyed everything we saw. John especially liked the carpentry and closely inspected the intricate carvings on the furniture.

After a long day, John and I visited the nearby bakery for our favorite pastries. This was the only place we found in China that served brewed coffee and this old sailor appreciated his black coffee.

The next day was out first day alone in Shanghai. My terrible sense of direction convinced me that we needed to stay close to the hotel. Choosing the direction of nicer buildings, we set out.

First, the bakery for breakfast. Then traveled down the main street in front of the hotel, finding the first large cross-street. It was six lanes wide and for foot traffic only. A park on one end was filled with mothers with babies in carriages or running about. John was the center of their attention in his wheelchair, heavy coat, hat, and sunglasses.

As we shopped up and down the street, we felt all eyes on us. We saw no other Americans in any of our travels. There was some difficulty in finding out the exchange rate when we purchased anything. At one point, a lady walking by stopped and asked in perfect English, "I work at a bank and would be happy to help you with the exchange rate." All the people there were curious but polite and cheerful.

Taking a chance, we entered a tiny restaurant on a side street. We were rewarded by a delicious lunch of noodles and vegetables in a tasty sauce. Several patrons stopped eating and watched us. Some even sat in the aisle near us. Just stared like we were from another planet.

As we left, we asked the hostess for the location of the rest room. She was very friendly, and holding her tiny dog in her arms, walked us down the street, into a building, up to the fourth floor and pointed. A rest room with holes in the floor, no toilet paper or wash up sinks. In the hallway, I realized I didn't know what direction our street was. With trepidation, I left John with strict orders to stay. He sometimes came looking for me in a store.

Since each floor had several stores, I traveled the square building until I could see our street out the window. John was where I left him and now, we waited about thirty minutes until an elevator came that the wheelchair could fit into. We stopped at a restaurant with a pizza sign out front. There was no pizza. We were served only one hamburger. I had to get upset and approach the cook and point to the menu showing two fingers.

Finally arriving back at the hotel, I decided that maybe a taxi would be better tomorrow. It was John's ninetieth birthday. We had selected a ferry ride on the Huang Pu River then dinner nearby at a well-advertised restaurant on the twenty-eighth floor.

It was cold on the river, and thankfully we wore warm clothing. John was so animated along the trip, pointing out places he had been. Two women pointed to their camera and indicated they wanted to take our pictures. We were the center of attention there also.

The Blue Indigo Restaurant was the nicest part of our

trip. Directly on the Huang Pu River, it overlooked a light show of nearby skyscrapers. Arriving on the top floor, we were quickly whisked to a quiet table with black tablecloth and elegant silverware and dishes. The atmosphere was serene with faraway oriental music. We ordered our meal, and the server was fascinated by John celebrating his birthday at this restaurant.

The chef came over to meet John. He stayed for several minutes, telling us about coming there recently from Australia. Excusing himself to return to work, our server came over and asked us to select a knife for our steak. They were lined up in a box on velvet, much too nice to eat with, but when in Rome. Our steak was incredible. All the items were perfect, even my wine and his coffee. A small cake with a candle was served for our desert.

The maître di came over as we finished. He offered to take us to the penthouse bar for coffee and a view. He carried our coats and had a waiter push John's wheelchair. It was a fantastic view, and John certainly had a bird's eye view of the river. They allowed us to sit in plush chairs next to the window for as long as John wanted.

The taxi ride home wasn't long, but John was sound asleep soon after pulling away from the restaurant. The next morning, he didn't recall the ride home.

Today was our day to travel home. Breakfast in our bakery was first. Yoyo picked us up at the hotel at ten for our flight at two. As she got us settled in the airport after checking our luggage, she sat with us for a few minutes. She gave John a crayon picture that her four-year-old daughter, Lynn, had drawn for him. He then listened to Lynn singing happy birthday, the only words she knew in English. Tears streamed down his cheeks. He hugged Yoyo, thanking her for being so kind to us.

As the flight attendant had promised John on our flight to China, she had booked us in a bulkhead seat. We had plenty of leg room for John to get up often and stretch.

All the way to Atlanta, John relived the trip, talking excitedly about his favorite parts. Since we hadn't enjoyed many good meals in China, we were salivating for a big juicy hamburger with French fries. While waiting for our connecting flight in Atlanta, we feasted on good American food.

On the short flight to Myrtle Beach, we both relaxed. I was anxious to get home to my pets. He was tired but still excited about this momentous trip. I dropped him off at his apartment and made sure he was safe in bed. The next morning, I went over to unpack for him. Once dressed, he was ready to go out on the porch to his personal rocker, to tell all his friends about his adventures in China. Before I left, he was already talking about maybe taking another trip!

# CHAPTER 19
# DANUBE CRUISE

2016

Four months after our trip to China, John approached me. "I'd like to go to Germany to the Black Forest where Hitler was during the war. Since I'm German, I may have some relatives there. Can you go on the computer and find any of my relatives?"

At ninety and in failing health, it was hard to say no to his requests. If he was physically able, I would take him. The China trip was tiring for him, but every minute was an adventure. On his return he talked about the trip incessantly. He shared his scrapbook with everyone who would listen to his exploits which became more exaggerated with each telling.

He received his ancestry results and was happy when he found he was eight-five percent German. His relative search was not completed prior to the trip.

The river cruises are a relaxing way to travel and would be easiest for John. We would be in one place the entire time and could sight see from the upper deck if he wasn't up to bus tours. I booked a ten-day trip cruising the Danube River, beginning in Budapest, and finishing in Nuremberg. I sensed John knew he wouldn't be traveling much in the future. He was always laughing and entertaining a crowd with his stories of WWII and exploits as a young man and looked forward to new audiences.

In a mad flurry of buying him clothes and packing, we were off for a long plane trip. He wore his George Washington socks as usual. This time we left from Myrtle Beach on Delta to Atlanta. Then off to Paris on Air France on an overnight flight to Budapest, landing at noon. With his unstable diabetes, I had one carry-on bag with protein drinks, water, and juice in case of low blood sugar. At every airport I bought several sandwiches since he didn't like airplane food.

He wore his WWII LST 969 hat, his most prized possession which he earned in the Pacific theater. The hat always drew fellow military people from the crowd who thanked him for his service. Many shared experiences with him. He recalled events like they were yesterday. What he didn't remember, he embellished.

The staff of Viking was waiting for the passengers and seamlessly loaded us into a bus and off to the ship. John had several best friends before we even reached the ship.

John and I had adjoining rooms. When we arrived, I unpacked his things while he took a nap. I had all his medications in my room and brought them over morning and evening. I selected his wardrobe while he showered. He was meticulous and a snappy dresser with starched shirts and dress pants. He loved his new boat shoes for the trip.

The ship was like a miniature palace. The clean Scandinavian décor of polished light wood was accentuated by bright lighting. Our spacious rooms had a queen bed and large bathroom. The sliding glass doors in our rooms allowed us to enjoy the scenery. The staff was so helpful with John, assisting him to his room via the wheelchair. He knew the first names of several staff members and we hadn't even seen the dining room yet.

Our first night at dinner, John and I sat family style at a large round table with several passengers. The ship staff made sure he was comfortable and placed his wheelchair where it was accessible. I read the menu to him since his vision was diminished. When foods were buffet style, I selected his food and served him. Meanwhile, he entertained everyone. Out table was always the last in the dining room each night.

I promised he could have one glass of dark German beer. I brought a bottle of dark beer to the table and with great fanfare, he toasted the table with his first glass of beer in over twenty years. The other half of the bottle was on the table as I went up to get his dinner at the buffet. Thinking he was pretty slick, he finished the beer and emptied the rest of the bottle in his glass. When I returned, several glances from around the table tipped me off. I casually picked up his glass and placed his dinner in front of him. I got his raised eyebrows and a guilty smile.

The ship had designated tours every day with special tours available. John selected an afternoon with the Hungarian Horsemen, an afternoon making candy at an Austrian Sweet Delights candy store and an evening opera in Vienna from the list of special tours.

Watching him enjoying everything like a small child was so fulfilling. He needed to always use the wheelchair now due to shortness of breath, but it didn't diminish his ability to have a good time.

One of the passengers named Mike from Pittsburg formed a special bond with John and took over pushing the wheelchair. Mike and he were like two teen-aged boys, taking off and scouting on their own. John whispered that they had stopped to urinate under a bridge and laughed about that for days.

Every day there were bus tours to castles and city tours in the cities we visited. In the early evening we sat on the upper deck, relaxing in comfortable chairs as we quietly slid by scenic villages along the Danube River.

John's favorite outing was the Hungarian Horse show. These majestic black horses, similar to the Lipizzaner stallions, are the pride of Hungarians. They played an important part in their history. The horsemen were incredible. We watched them ride standing on the bare back of their horses, around a ring, flicking their whips, the wind blowing the long hair of the horses and the leather pants of the riders. With a glass of beer on their heads, around the ring they flew by the stands without spilling any of the beer. After the show John had the opportunity to meet a couple of the riders and have his picture taken with them.

Vienna is an elegant city. The multilevel buildings have ornate black metal balconies with colorful baskets of hanging flowers. On our tour we passed Vienna's art museum, a castle, home of composers Strauss and Mozart. The city itself has scattered parks and footpaths leading to cafes where we sampled Viennese sweet treats. Out tour included the Opera House and St. Stephen's Cathedral.

One afternoon, John and I wandered into the city to the candy shop where we would learn to make candy. Donned with aprons and a chef hat, along with four others from the ship, we began our lessons. We learned to make intricate hard candies and lollipops. John was so proud of his finished products. We wrapped them for the trip home to give to friends.

I think John selected the opera for me. Long staircases in the elegant opera house were imposing when we arrived, but fortunately there was an elevator. John wore his black suit, white shirt with French cuffs, a bright red tie, and a red carnation in his lapel. He looked so handsome.

I was concerned about the acoustics with the small concert hall and high ceilings but after the first note, the sound was perfect. Four young people came onto a central stage. Three violins and a cello. The music was magical. One young man had a solo that pulled at my heart and made me want to cry it was so emotional. He looked like a teenager. So much talent. We were then treated to three ballerinas who used every inch of the small stage with grace and beauty. John loved the evening and gave me a big hug as we left. It was a wonderful evening for both of us.

A special evening was part of the tour for everyone on the ship. Our large gathering took up an entire part of a garden. We sat at long picnic tables and enjoyed an age-old tradition celebrating the year's harvest. Waiters and waitresses were dressed in traditional costumes. An accordion player and singer entertained us. John casually got up and put his arm around the waist of the waitress. He pulled her next to the two singers and proceeded to sing with the group. Of course, the waitress was attractive, with a low bodice.

He is such a flirt and thinks he's a lady's man. He got a lot of cheers from our group. I whispered to him that if he had some silver dollars in his pocket and felt better, he could probably talk that waitress into a "poke". I loved to see him have such a good time, but that night tired him out, causing increased shortness of breath.

We arrived in Germany near the end of our trip. John and I sat on the front deck of the ship as we traveled through the locks. We both marveled at the ingenuity. We took it easy that day and stayed on ship. The evening dinner had local dancers entertain us before dinner. After another delicious meal, John entertained for a while, but we left earlier than usual. As soon as he had his medications, he was fast asleep.

Our last morning, I woke John and helped him dress. His breathing was noticeably worsening. I persuaded him to take a cab into Nuremberg that day and take his wheelchair. Part of what he wanted from this trip was to see Germany. In the village, I pushed him around the large square, shopped a little for German mugs and refrigerator magnets for us and for friends, and after about two hours, it was time to leave. John took a nap back at the ship, dressed for a short dinner and back to bed after his medications.

We left early the next morning. It was hard work for him to get ready. I had his clothes out and his suitcase packed. Mike and he said their goodbyes and we were off to the airport.

To say that it was a long difficult trip home would be an understatement. John's blood sugar kept dropping and he didn't want to eat. He got into the rest room on the plane and had trouble opening the door. I had a soda for him to drink when we finally got him out.

By the time we got to Atlanta, I wondered if I had to take him to the hospital there or chance the ride to Myrtle Beach. He refused food in Atlanta. He didn't recall being there the next day. We arrived in Myrtle Beach and went by taxi to the emergency room where he was admitted for his congestive heart failure and unstable diabetes.

When he arrived back at his apartment a few days later, he was much improved. He did decide that he should consider a living arrangement with medical supervision. He picked a facility he liked after a thorough visit and lots of questions, especially about their food. He even insisted on trying lunch while we were visiting. He would find new audiences.

John visited his family in Illinois in September. I took him to see everyone and to check on the stone he had ordered for his grave. The gravestone was red marble and larger than the other monuments on the family plot. It didn't surprise me that he had the Lonesome Dove engraved under his name and birth date. He wanted to see it for himself. His family relations were not improved when he had the gravestone company place the stone on a site that had been reserved for another family member. During the visit he managed to smooth over past issues and left everyone wishing him well.

Two months after his trip to Illinois, John's diabetes became worse. In November 2018, he fought his last battle. At the service in Illinois with his family in attendance, there was a Mason ceremony as he had earned the highest degree in that organization. His nephew, also a Mason, performed the ceremony.

I was sad, but my mind wandered. I could visualize John,

sitting with Gus and Lorna in the Lonesome Dove Saloon. There were beers all around, and John was entertaining them with his stories. I knew he had a deck of cards and silver dollars jingling in his pocket.

169

**THE END**